CHRISTMAS IN MY HEART

6

JOE L. WHEELER

REVIEW AND HERALD® PUBLISHING ASSOCIATION
HAGERSTOWN, MD 21740

This book was
Edited by Jeannette R. Johnson
Designed by Patricia S. Wegh
Cover illustrations by Superstock/Currier & Ives
Woodcut illustrations are from the library of Joe L. Wheeler
Typeset: 11/12 Goudy

PRINTED IN U.S.A.

01 00 99 98 97   5 4 3 2

R&H Cataloging Service
Wheeler, Joe L., 1936-   comp.
    Christmas in my heart. Book 6.

    1. Christmas stories, American.   I. Title:
Christmas in my heart. Book 6.

                813.101833

ISBN 0-8280-1310-1

Dedication

PENNY ESTES WHEELER

Had it not been for her, some six plus years ago, the great ministry of Judeo-Christian stories (which has since commandeered my life) would, most likely, never have been.

Even the title, *Christmas in My Heart,* is hers.

So whatever it will become, wherever it will go, whatever impact for good it will have, much of the credit ought to go to her, my long-time acquisitions editor and friend.

To order additional copies of Joe Wheeler's book call **1-800-765-6955**

Visit us at www.rhpa.org

Acknowledgments

"From Saint Nicholas to Santa Claus" (Introduction), by Joseph Leininger Wheeler. Copyright 1997. Printed by permission of the author.

"Small Things," by Margaret E. Sangster, Jr. Published in Sangster's *The Littlest Orphan and Other Christmas Stories*, Round Table Press, New York, 1928. If anyone can provide knowledge of origin and first publication source of this old story, please relay this information to Joe L. Wheeler, in care of Review and Herald Publishing Association.

"The Servant Candle," by Terry Beck. Published in *Virtue*, November-December, 1995. Copyright 1995. Printed by permission of the author.

"Clorinda's Gifts," by Lucy Maud Montgomery. Published in *Christmas With Anne and Other Holiday Stories*, McClelland & Stewart, Inc., Toronto, Canada. Copyright 1995. Compilation, introduction, and edited by David Macdonald, Ruth Macdonald, and Rea Wilmshurst. Reprinted by permission of McClelland & Stewart, Inc.

"So Cold, So Far From Home," by Maimu Veedler. Copyright 1997. Printed by permission of the author.

"Christmas on the Homestead in 1894," by Rosina Kiehlbauch. Reprinted by permission of the American Historical Society of Germans From Russia, Lincoln, Nebraska.

"The Miraculous Staircase," by Arthur Gordon. Published in *Guideposts Magazine*, May 1956, and in *The Guideposts Christmas Treasury*, Guideposts, New York, 1972; also published in Gordon's book, *A Touch of Wonder*, Fleming H. Revell Company, New York, 1974. Reprinted by permission of the author.

"The Stuffed Kitten," by Mae Hurley Ashworth. Published in *The Town Journal*, December 1953. If anyone can provide knowledge of origin and first publication source of this story, please relay this information to Joe L. Wheeler, in care of Review and Herald Publishing Association.

"Matthew, Mark, Luke, and John," by Pearl S. Buck. Copyright 1966. Reprinted by permission of Harold Ober Associates, Inc.

"Their Best Christmas," by Hartley F. Dailey. Copyright 1997. Printed by permission of the author.

"A Stolen Christmas," by Charles M. Sheldon. Published in *Fifty Years of Christmas*, Rinehart & Co., New York, 1951. Reprinted by permission of Christian Herald Association.

"To See Again," by Gary B. Swanson. Published in *Insight*, Dec. 15, 1984. Copyright 1984. Reprinted by permission of the author.

"Bid the Tapers Twinkle," by Bess Streeter Aldrich. Published in Aldrich's *Journey Into Christmas*, Appleton

Contents

The Friendly Beasts
12th Century Carol

Jesus our brother, kind and good,
Was humbly born in a stable rude,
And the friendly beasts around Him stood;
Jesus our brother, kind and good.

"I," said the donkey, shaggy and brown,
"I carried His mother up hill and down,
I carried her safely to Bethlehem town;
I," said the donkey, shaggy and brown.

"I," said the cow, all white and red,
"I gave Him my manger for His bed,
I gave Him my hay to pillow His head;
I," said the cow, all white and red.

"I," said the sheep, with curly horn,
"I gave Him my wool for His blanket warm,
He wore my coat on Christmas morn;
I," said the sheep, with curly horn.

"I," said the dove, from the rafters high,
"Cooed Him to sleep, my mate and I,
We cooed Him to sleep, my mate and I;
I," said the dove, from the rafters high.

And every beast, by some good spell,
In the stable dark was glad to tell
Of the gift he gave Immanuel,
The gift he gave Immanuel.

From Saint Nicholas to Santa Claus

Joseph Leininger Wheeler

All my life, I've wondered how in the world one gets from Saint Nicholas to Santa Claus. For that matter, who *was* Saint Nicholas, and why do we still remember him? I decided to find out. And what did I discover?

Well, I discovered that Saint Nicholas himself is so beclouded in myth that it is almost impossible to separate fact from fiction. What *is* clear, however, is that he is one of the dominant figures of the past 1600 years—and each age has found it necessary to reinvent him. In one way or another, all of us yearn toward ideals. In that respect, Catholics have the jump on the rest of us, because, traditionally, Catholic babies have been named for the saint on whose birthday they were born. That saint becomes an ideal to grow toward—well, the *perception* of who that saint was, the qualities that his or her life represented. And Saint Nicholas has represented that ideal more than any other religious figure since the time of Christ.

Machiavelli noted in *The Prince* that perception is more significant than reality. In ruling a people, he points out, it is more important that a prince be *perceived* as moral than to *be* moral. It is therefore more important to discover how Saint Nicholas has been *perceived* over the centuries than to know who he really *was*.

But let's start with what we *do* know for certain. The answer is, nothing. We can capsulize, though, what most scholars *believe* to be true (but even this is sketchy):

◆ He was born around 280 A.D. in Patara, Lycia, a sort of oriental Switzerland. Twenty-six towns stretch between the seacoast and the Taurus Mountains in what is modern Turkey. If you're looking for it on the map, it's the peninsula that separates the Gulf of Makri from the Gulf of Adalia. Saint Paul knew Lycia well, converting many to Christianity here. Other Christian converts from Saint Paul's evangelism in Antioch later settled here as well.

◆ His parents were rather wealthy, devout Christians.

◆ An uncle was a Christian bishop.

◆ Nicholas was precocious; deeply religious as he grew up.

◆ His parents died in a plague epidemic.

◆ Upon the death of the incumbent, Nicholas was ordained Bishop of Myra.

◆ He was supposedly one of the 318 bishops called by Constantine to the famous Council of Nicaea that convened May 20 to July 25, 325 A.D.

◆ During the Emperor Diocletian's persecution of the Christians, Nicholas was imprisoned and tortured. In 303 A.D., Diocletian decreed that Christian churches be destroyed, their books burned, and all civil liberties taken away.

◆ Nicholas died on December 6, 341 A.D.

Now let's turn to a hash of truth, legend, and speculation—all fascinating ingredients for mythhood—out of which was forged the Cult of Saint Nicholas.

◆ Nicholas was born to an infertile woman on the condition that he be consecrated to a priestly ministry, similar to the experience of the Old Testament's Hannah, mother of Samuel, and the New Testament's Elizabeth, mother of John the Baptist.

◆ The baby Nicholas was so precocious that he stood up in his bathtub almost as soon as he was born, and he didn't demand his mother's breast on fast days, Wednesdays, or Fridays, except after sunset. This spiritual precociousness continued through his growing up years. He was ordained when he was only 19 (no doubt through the good offices of his uncle, bishop of a nearby bishopric, who was his spiritual mentor).

◆ While Nicholas was still young (around 19), a wealthy neighbor, who had three beautiful daughters of marriageable age, lost almost everything. Without money for dowries, there were only two likely alternatives: he would have to sell them as slaves, or sell them into prostitution.

When young Nicholas heard of the situation, he was appalled. After thinking about the matter, one night he tossed a purse of gold through their open window, then hurried away. The purse contained enough money to marry off the oldest girl and leave a little to live on. When that gold was almost gone, Nicholas tossed in a second purse, and the second daughter was married off. When even that money was about gone, Nicholas tossed a third bag of gold through their window. But this time the watching father ran out and caught Nicholas before he would get away. Thus the third daughter was saved. Nicholas swore the father to secrecy.

◆ Following the example of his bishop uncle, Nicholas decided to visit a number of the places Christians considered sacred. Wanting to be alone to meditate about his life ministry, he boarded an Egyptian ship that also carried other pilgrims.

During the first night, Nicholas dreamed that the devil was cutting the ropes that held the ship's mast. The next morning he told the sailors to expect a severe storm, but they should not worry—God would see them through. Sure enough, a violent storm struck during which many sailors despaired of ever seeing land again. One seaman, who climbed the main mast to tighten the ropes, slipped during the descent and fell to the deck, dying on impact. When Nicholas prayed that the Lord would bring the seaman back to life, miraculously, the man began breathing again.

There are a number of other accounts of miraculous experiences involving seamen.

◆ After becoming Bishop of Myra, a famine brought his people to the brink of starvation. Providentially, a fleet of grain ships from Antioch was blown off course by tremendous winds and forced to moor at Patara. Bishop Nicholas approached the commander and asked him to leave 100 bushels of grain from each ship. When the commander resisted (understandably), the good bishop pointed out that the cargo had already been weighed at Antioch and promised to stand good for the act. He guaranteed there would be no problems for the commander down the line.

So the grain was transferred. And when the ships reached their destination, not one bushel of grain was found to be missing. This grain enabled the people of Myra to survive two more years of famine and still have enough left for seed to plant new crops.

◆ During this same famine the bishop stopped at the home of a man who was suspected of cannibalism. When the meat was brought to the table, the bishop told his host he had been found out and proceeded to find the dismembered bodies of three boys in a tub (some versions say it was a barrel). By praying to God the bishop was instrumental in bringing the boys back to life and restoring them to their mother.

◆ In a triptych of a miracle, three young men were unjustly condemned to death on perjurious charges by a crooked judge. Upon hearing of this, the bishop hurried to the execution, bringing along three visiting officers of Emperor Constantine. Just before the sword dropped, the bishop struck down the sword with his staff, reproached the guilty judge, and had the men released. The three officers went on to complete their mission, then returned to Constantinople to receive the plaudits of their emperor and the people. However, certain envious men accused the officers of failing in their mission and of plotting against the emperor. They were cast into prison and condemned to death on the basis of perjured testimony.

The night before their execution, they prayed all night. They entreated God to save them, in the name of Bishop Nicholas, who had been instrumental in saving the lives of those other unjustly accused men.

That same night Constantine had a dream. A stately figure came to the emperor and said, "Arise, emperor. Rise quickly! You must free the three men whom you have condemned to death. If you do not do as I say God will involve you in a war that will result in your own death."

The emperor, not sure if he was asleep or awake, demanded to know the identity of the break-in visitor.

"I am Nicholas, the Bishop of Myra, and God has sent me to tell you that these three men must be freed without delay."

The bishop also appeared in a dream to Evlavios, Constantine's imperial Chancellor, demanding to know why he had allowed himself to be bribed, and why he was condemning three innocent men to death.

"Free them at once, or I shall ask God to take your life!" the bishop demanded.

No sooner did Evlavios awaken than he was summoned to the palace by the emperor. The three condemned generals (Ursos, Nepotianos, and Herpylion) were also brought to the palace, and Constantine demanded to know what magic they were using to bring the same dream to both him and the chancellor.

After being convinced that it was no setup, Nepotianos told how, as result of their experience with Bishop Nicholas, they had appealed to God, in the bishop's name, to save them. Constantine was so impressed that he freed them and sent them to the bishop with valuable gifts for the Cathedral of Myra, instructing them to dedicate the rest of their lives to the church.

◆ Nicholas was one of the 318 bishops summoned by Emperor Constantine to the great Council of Nicaea. Constantine had trod a very dangerous road en route to preeminence in the empire. He had fought many battles and survived much intrigue. Along the way, like Saul on the way to Damascus, he had had a conversion experience. The Vision of the Flaming Cross appeared in the noonday sky (some say in a dream at night). Constantine became a Christian and, ever after, used the flaming cross symbol in all his battles.

After years of consolidating power, Constantine turned to matters that had been shunted aside in his long march to the throne. With the 313 A.D. Edict of Milan, Christians had been taken off the list of the dis-enfranchised, but it was not until the execution of his last rival, Licinius, in 325, that Constantine at last ruled supreme in both the Eastern Roman Empire and the Western Roman Empire.

A year later, feeling that Rome was too pagan to serve as the seat of a Christian empire, he announced that he had been told in a dream to move the capital to an entirely new site, Byzantium, on the Bosporus where East meets West. The cornerstone of Constantinople was laid in 326, and the new capital was dedicated in 330.

But before this move took place, Constantine de-termined that something had to be done about the splintering of the Christian church. So long as persecu-tion continued Christians remained united; but as soon as persecution ceased, Christian began turning on Christian, threatening the stability of the empire itself. Consequently, in 325 Constantine convened 318 bish-ops from East and West (but predominantly East) at Nicaea, a beautiful city in Bithynia on Lake Ascania, a short distance from Byzantium, and near Nicomedia, the seaside summer palace of the emperor.

But now, Constantine was all business. Not only was

he the supreme political leader, he was also the supreme religious leader. Constantine's power was absolute, and here he sat in regal splendor, enthroned above the 318 bishops, 159 on each side of him. Donatists, who believed that only the morally pure were worthy of inclusion in their churches, were also present—fierce, unyielding, and ultraconservative. On the other hand was the group led by Arius, Presbyter of Alexandria. Their incendiary philosophical agenda represented an ideological powder keg far more than did the ultra-righteous Donatists, for the Arians denied the divinity of Christ.

And poor Constantine brought all these men, plus the centrists (those who kind of waffled around in the middle somewhere), together and asked them to achieve consensus!

Supposedly, the debate got so heated that fiery Nicholas, a lion of God when he became angry, temporarily forgot he was in the imperial presence and rushed up to Arius and *slapped him in the face!* To attack someone in the presence of the emperor was punishable by death. The emperor turned the matter over to the bishops, who voted to strip Nicholas of his priestly robes and haul him off to prison.

Eventually, the Council stumbled to a consensus that pleased no one, but it staved off disaster. Out of this ambiguous synthesis came the Nicene Creed, that itself unleashed a storm, but the forces of centricity had won, and Arianism and Donatism had received deadly blows from which they never completely recovered. But the struggle would last for centuries. Nicholas, having given the slap to one of the "losers," was released and reinstated.

◆ Nicholas was also a lion where the cult of Artemis (or Diana) was concerned, and waged a lifelong war against them and their temples. Many early Christians still retained a soft spot for the allure of Artemis (daughter of Zeus and Leto, twin sister and counterpart of Apollo). Today we may laugh at the likelihood that her worship would challenge Christianity, but it was no laughing matter to the bishop, for Artemis was one of the few supreme forces in his world.

She was the goddess of chastity, childbirth, and the protectress of young men and young women. Like her brother, Apollo, she not only dealt death but also purified and healed. She was the goddess of fertility, of agriculture, of the harvest, and of seamen. Often called the Virgin Goddess, and later the Moon Goddess, she was associated with the torch, the bear, the boar, the deer, the dog, the goat, the lion, and the chase.

Her chief festival occurred in the spring, at which time Greek-type games and contests were held. As time passed, these celebrations lost their earlier moral tone and became orgiastic. All boys were brought to her temples to be consecrated to her. On a certain day all the boys would cut off their hair and dedicate it to her.

Perhaps an analogy may help us better identify with Saint Nicholas's fight against Artemis. Today's counterparts—and antagonists who are just as serious—would be astrology and New Age philosophy (apparently, very, very rarely is anything ever *really new*).

This is about all we know about the "real" Nicholas. From these incidents was built the legend of Saint Nicholas and all his spiritual and secular godchildren.

And Each Age Reinvented Him

From all appearances, the good bishop was not widely known in his time. In fact, he was not even mentioned by name in historical accounts of the Council of Nicaea. He lived and died in his own narrow world of Myra. But after his death, stories, such as the one about the dowries for the three beautiful girls, came to light, and gradually he become legendary in Myra, and his memory was revered.

Complicating things even more was the fact that there was another Nicholas. This Nicholas, Abbot of the Zion Monastery near Myra, later became Bishop of Pinara in the Sixth Century. He was a great traveler and, inevitably, some of his achievements and exploits were stirred into the Saint Nicholas mix.

As we have seen, paganism was no mean antagonist. Not surprisingly, early Christians gradually developed a counterforce, a mythology of devout and principled men and women Christians could identify with. In Nicholas of Myra they found a perfect candidate, and ever so gradually his mystique grew.

A key factor was the abduction of his remains from the Myra Cathedral to Bari, Italy, ostensibly to save the remains from the Saracens. The kidnappers and the remains arrived there May 9, 1098. A great basilica was built over them by Pope Urban II; and from that time on West, as well as East, accepted Nicholas.

But in 911 A.D., before those relics were removed, Prince Oleg of the Russian principality of Kiev, signed a treaty of friendship with the Byzantine rulers that was later solidified by marriage into the imperial family. As part of all this, precious relics, Saint Nicholas's among them, were sent to Kiev. And over time, Saint Nicholas became the patron saint of all Russia, with even emperors taking his name. Other names derived from Nicholas include Niccolo, Nicole, Colin, Colette, Niklaus, Niklas, and Claus.

By the twelfth and thirteenth centuries Saint Nicholas had become third (in the Catholic world) only to Christ and the Virgin Mary, in terms of veneration. Not surprisingly, considering his association with the sea, Saint Nicholas became the patron saint of all seamen. And for other reasons we have already noted, he also became the ultimate protector of children, marriageable daughters, the falsely accused, endangered travelers, farmers, bankers, pawnbrokers, traveling students, barren wives, pirating vandals, and even thieves! The fighting bishop, the most human of all saints, became the patron saint of nearly *everybody*.

Many of the medieval morality plays had to do with the life and ministry of Saint Nicholas. These early dramas, simplistic and filled with raucous humor and buffoonery, gradually altered the perception of Saint Nicholas from one of severe piety to one of at least slight humor. These plays were the real antecedents of today's short stories, novels, dramas, and celluloid media forms. From very early on, artists painted him again and again. In the process, he became stereotyped, complete with episcopal habit, mitre, cope, crozier, staff, book, and either three balls or three purses (the latter having to do with the tripartite stories of the three sisters and the three unjustly accused men).

Interestingly, thanks to the Medici of Florence, the symbol of the three balls went worldwide. Apparently, these Medici bankers (Europe's first), in searching for a

symbol for financial transactions based on mutual trust, were convinced that Saint Nicholas would be the ultimate metaphor. So it was that their family heraldic symbol of the three balls became used by bankers everywhere. Today, however, the symbol is used only by pawnshops. What a comedown!

A frozen-in-time depiction of Saint Nicholas's place in society is a sixteenth century painting by the Dutch master, Jan Steen. (Saint Nicholas has long been the patron saint of Holland and, later, Dutch-settled New York). In the painting are 10 people: a father, a mother, a grandmother, and seven children. The oldest boy is pointing to the place under the chimney mantel where Saint Nicholas's presents are to come down—good children receiving sweets and toys; bad children receiving bundles of switches.

So December 6, the anniversary of his death, came to be known as St. Nicholas Day. In many parts of Europe this day is the happiest of the year for children. Shops are filled with biscuits, gingerbread (many times representing the saint), sugar images, and toys. On the Eve of Saint Nicholas, Saint Nicholas look-alikes, complete with mitre and staff, inquire about children's behavior. If the report is good, a benediction is pronounced and an appropriate reward is promised for the following day.

Before going to bed children put out their shoes and leave hay, straw, or a carrot for Saint Nicholas's horse or donkey. When they awake on Saint Nicholas Day, if they've been good, the fodder is gone and sweets or toys are in their place. If they've been bad, the fodder is left untouched, and a rod or switches are left to encourage better behavior in the future.

In Germanic countries Saint Nicholas is impressive indeed. Attired as a bishop, gray-haired with a flowing beard, gold embroidered cape, glittering mitre, and pastoral staff, he sits astride a big white horse. He's followed by such fearsome creatures as a Pelsnickel, Black Peter, or Klaubauf, all serving as the punishers of bad children. But those who know their catechism are rewarded by another attendant who passes out candies, cookies, and other goodies.

Interestingly, while leaders of the Protestant Reformation were comparatively successful at eliminating the role of saints in Protestant Europe, they had little success here, for Saint Nicholas stubbornly refused to go away. In the end, Protestants adopted him too.

Saint Nicholas Comes to America

A large number of the Europeans who resettled in America brought the traditions of Saint Nicholas with them. By then some artists were depicting him with a reindeer instead of a horse, and sometimes with both. Until the early nineteenth century, however, Saint Nicholas was almost invariably perceived in a spiritual rather than a secular sense. Therefore, Saint Nicholas Day meshed well with the 24 days of the Advent.

In America, the transition from Saint to Santa occurred with amazing rapidity. The Dutch, who called Saint Nicholas "Sinta Claes," brought him with them when they settled in New York.

Another factor in the transition was John Pintard, founder of the New York Historical Society. A key figure in making Washington's birthday and July 4 na-

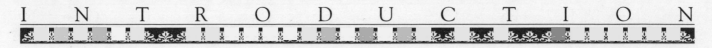
tional holidays, he organized a Saint Nicholas celebration in 1810.

A third factor in transforming Saint Nicholas into Santa Claus was Washington Irving (1783-1859). In 1809 Irving had been nominated for membership in the New York Historical Society. Irving created the mythology for Saint Nicholas's change in his hilarious spoof, *Dietrich Knickerbocker's History of New York*, first published in 1809. Irving's genius was such that readers of the mock epic found it almost impossible to separate what was true from what was not. And it was read and chuckled over across the nation, as well as in England and the Empire, where Irving first attained real fame. (He was the first American author to be feted as an equal by England's literati). Saint Nicholas/Santa Claus appears 25 times in the work. One passage is particularly noteworthy:

"And the sage Oloffe dreamed a dream—and lo, the good Saint Nicholas came riding over the tops of the trees, in that selfsame wagon wherein he brings his yearly presents to children, and he descended hard by where the heroes of Communipaw had made their late repast. And he lit his pipe by the fire, and sat himself down and smoked; and as he smoked the smoke from his pipe ascended into the air and spread like a cloud overhead. And Oloffe bethought him, and he hastened and climbed up to the top of one of the tallest trees, and saw that the smoke spread over a great extent of country—and as he considered it more attentively, he fancied that the great volume of smoke assumed a variety of marvelous forms, where in dim obscurity he saw shadowed out palaces and domes and lofty spires, all of which lasted but a moment, and then faded away, until the whole rolled off, and nothing but the green woods were left. And when Saint Nicholas had smoked his pipe, he twisted it in his hat-band, and laying his finger beside his nose, gave the astonished Van Kortlandt a very significant look, then mounting his wagon, he returned over the tree-tops and disappeared" (Ebon, p. 94).*

Enter next the distinguished clergyman, Dr. Clement Clarke Moore (1779-1863), Hebraic Scholar at New York's General Theological Seminary. As Christmas 1822 approached, Dr. Moore, an accomplished poet, decided to write a present for his children. Suddenly the concept came to him: to bring to life, via poetry, Irving's unique depiction of Saint Nicholas. Saint Nicholas had always before been depicted as thin, but Irving, in order to elicit more humor, had transformed him into a jolly fat man.

So it was that Moore put all Irving's ingredients together, added some of his own, and on the evening of December 23, 1822, he read "A Visit From Saint Nicholas" to his children. That might have been the end of it had not a lady visitor been there that night. She begged a copy and had it published anonymously in the *Sentinel* of Troy, New York, at Christmas time, 1823.

───────

I am deeply indebted to Martin Ebon's fascinating Saint Nicholas: Life and Legend, Harper & Row, 1975, which has been invaluable in helping me grasp the significance of the Saint Nicholas phenomenon. I also found Eugene R. Whitmore's Saint Nicholas, Bishop of Myra, private printing, 1944, and Clement A. Miles' Christmas in Ritual and Tradition, Christian and Pagan, T. Fisher Unwin, London, 1912, 1968, to be helpful.

A Visit From St. Nicholas

'Twas the night before Christmas when all through
    the house
Not a creature was stirring, not even a mouse;
The stockings were hung by the chimney with care,
In hopes that St. Nicholas soon would be there;
The children were nestled all snug in their beds,
While visions of sugar-plums danced through their
        heads;
And Mamma in her kerchief, and I in my cap,
Had just settled our brains for a long winter's nap—
When out on the lawn there rose such a clatter,
I sprang from my bed to see what was the matter.
Away to the window I flew like a flash.
Tore open the shutters and threw up the sash.
The moon, on the breast of the new-fallen snow,
Gave a luster of mid-day to objects below,
When, what to my wondering eyes should appear
But a miniature sleigh, and eight tiny reindeer,
With a little old driver, so lively and quick,
I knew in a moment it must be St. Nick.

More rapid than eagles his coursers they came,
And he whistled, and shouted, and called them
        by name;
"Now, Dasher! now, Dancer! now, Prancer and Vixen!
On, Comet! on, Cupid! on, Dunder and Blitzen—
To the top of the porch, to the top of the wall!
Now, dash away, dash away, dash away all!"
As leaves that before the wild hurricane fly,
When they meet with an obstacle, mount to the sky,
So, up to the house top the coursers they flew,

With a sleigh full of toys—and St. Nicholas, too.

And then in a twinkling I heard on the roof,
The prancing and pawing of each little hoof.
As I drew in my head, and was turning around,
Down the chimney St. Nicholas came with a bound.
He was dressed all in fur from his head to his foot,
And his clothes were all tarnished with ashes and soot;
A bundle of toys he had flung on his back.
And he looked like a peddler just opening his pack.
His eyes how they twinkled! his dimples how merry!
His cheeks were like roses, his nose like a cherry;
His droll little mouth was drawn up like a bow,
And the beard on his chin was as white as the snow.
The stump of a pipe he held tight in his teeth,
And the smoke, it encircled his head like a wreath.

He had a broad face, and a little round belly,
That shook when he laughed, like a bowl full of jelly.
He was chubby and plump—a right jolly old elf;
And I laughed when I saw him, in spite of myself.
A wink of his eye, and a twist of his head,
Soon gave me to know I had nothing to dread.
He spoke not a word, but went straight to his work,
And filled all the stockings; then turned with a jerk,
And laying his finger aside of his nose,
And giving a nod, up the chimney he rose.
He sprang to his sleigh, to his team gave a whistle,
And away they all flew like the down of a thistle;
But I heard him exclaim, ere he drove out of sight,

        "Happy Christmas to all,
        and to all a good night!"

17

In reprints and anthologies, the words of Moore's poem entered the language: "'Twas the night before Christmas," "visions of sugar-plums," "Now, Dasher! now, Dancer! now, Prancer and Vixen!" and "a sleigh full of toys," "a bundle of toys he had flung on his back," "a right jolly old elf" who "filled all the stockings" and "up the chimney he rose" to enter "his sleigh." (Ebon, 98).

It would be 22 years before Dr. Moore would admit publicly that he had written the poem. What would people say? Imagine! A divinity professor writing such things! Finally, in 1844, Moore legitimized this brain child in a collection of his poetry that he published.

Moore's poem, building on Irving as a base, stirs in Pelznickel in the creation of Saint Nicholas's fur costume (see "A Pennsylvania Deutsch Christmas" in *Christmas in My Heart*, book 4). From both Sweden and America he derived the reindeer image (the reindeer names are both Germanic and English).

But the poem by itself would quite possibly not have survived without the reinforcement of German-born Thomas Nast (1840-1902), the greatest cartoonist of the nineteenth Century. Although Nast is remembered most as the one force powerful enough to topple New York's corrupt Boss Tweed and Tammany Hall, his range was much wider than politics. He had a genius for image creation. (It was he who came up with the donkey symbol for the Democratic Party and elephant for the Republican Party.)

Starting in the early 1860s, Nast began a series of woodcut illustrations depicting Saint Nicholas/Santa Claus for the Christmas issues of *Harpers Illustrated Monthly Magazines*. He derived his ideas from Irving,

from Moore's poem, and from his own Germanic cultural heritage. These woodcut illustrations circulated everywhere. Large prints were made of them as well. The visual impact cannot be overstated.

The most widely publicized and circulated editorial of all time was written anonymously by Frances Pharcellus Church and was published by *The New York Sun* on September 21, 1897. An 8-year-old girl, Virginia O'Hanlon, who had always believed in the existence of Santa Claus, found her beliefs challenged by children she knew. When even her father's answers seemed evasive, she turned to the family court of last resort, the *Sun* question and answer column.

After giving her age, she posed this question in her letter to the editor: "Some of my little friends say there is no Santa Claus. Papa says, 'If you see it in the *Sun*, it's so.' Please tell me the truth, is there a Santa Claus?"
—Virginia O'Hanlon

As day after day passed and Virginia saw no answer to her letter in the question and answer column, she grew more and more disconsolate. Then one day Dr. O'Hanlon called his daughter from his downtown office. This was a *big* event, for telephones were then used only for emergencies or major news. "Virginia," he told her, "they *did* answer your letter. They gave you a whole editorial!"

The editorial was entitled, "Yes, Virginia, There Is a Santa Claus!" and read as follows:

"We take pleasure in answering at once and thus prominently the communication below, expressing at the same time our great satisfaction that its faithful author is numbered among the friends of the *Sun*."

After giving the text of the girl's letter, the editorial

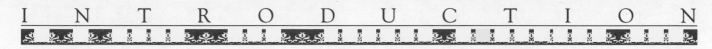

continued, "Virginia, your little friends are wrong. They have been affected by the skepticism of a skeptical age. They do not believe except they see. They think that nothing can be which is not comprehensible by their little minds.

"All minds, Virginia, whether they be men's or children's, are little. In this great universe of ours man is a mere insect, an ant, in his intellect, as compared with the boundless world about him, as measured by the intelligence capable of grasping the whole of truth and knowledge.

"Yes, Virginia, there is a Santa Claus. He exists as certainly as love and generosity and devotion exist, and you know that they abound and give to your life its highest beauty and joy. Alas! How dreary would be the world if there were no Santa Claus! It would be as dreary as if there were no Virginias.

"There would be no childlike faith then, no poetry, no romance to make tolerable this existence. We should have no enjoyment except in sense and sight. The eternal light with which childhood fills the world would be extinguished.

"Not believe in Santa Claus! You might as well not believe in fairies! You might get your papa to hire men to watch in all the chimneys on Christmas Eve to catch Santa Claus, but even if they did not see Santa Claus coming down, what would that prove?

"Nobody sees Santa Claus, but that is no sign that there is no Santa Claus. The most real things in the world are those that neither children nor men can see. Did you ever see fairies dancing on the lawn? Of course not, but that's no proof that they are not there. Nobody

19

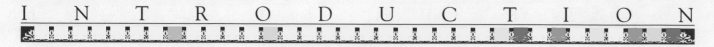
can conceive or imagine all the wonders that are unseen and unseeable in the world.

"You tear apart a baby's rattle and see what makes the noise inside, but there is a veil covering the unseen world which not the strongest man, nor even the united strength of all the strongest men that ever lived, could tear apart.

"Only faith, fancy, poetry, love, romance, can push aside that curtain and view and picture the supernatural beauty and glory beyond. Is it all real? Ah, Virginia, in all this world there is nothing else real and abiding.

"No Santa Claus! Thank God, he lives, and he lives forever. A thousand years from now, Virginia, nay, ten times ten thousand years from now, he will continue to make glad the heart of childhood" (Ebon, pp. 106, 107).

Ironically, Mr. Church had initially been anything but happy about being given the assignment of responding to Virginia's letter, for he was known as being a cynical, crusty fellow, who had been a Civil War correspondent and had no children of his own. Nevertheless, he penned this remarkable editorial. It went *everywhere* and did much to validate the place of Santa Claus/Saint Nicholas in American culture. Sadly, the editorial has sailed along without giving credit to the man who wrote it.

And one additional name needs to be included: Haddon Sundblom, the artist whose depictions of Santa Claus on Coca Cola ads were so splendidly done, and which were reproduced by the millions. These brought the 1600-year development of the Nicholas image to its conclusion, to our perception of him today.

So what does it all mean?

As we have already noted, each age has reinvented Saint Nicholas in order to adapt him to its unique needs. When Christianity was new and education almost nonexistent, a deeply spiritual and mystical depiction was natural. That state of affairs continued for nearly a millennium, through the Crusades and the great Age of Faith that inspired Europe's soaring Gothic cathedrals.

But with the Renaissance came a more secular world, as well as the beginnings of literacy. After centuries of Catholics slaughtering Protestants (and Protestants slaughtering Catholics), by the millions, all in the name of the same God, it was difficult to avoid disillusion. Where *was* God in all this blood and gore? The logical result was a new cynicism about religion. Hence, the transition of Saint Nicholas from an austere saint to one with a sense of humor to a figure capable of being attacked, even ridiculed.

Then came the seismic eighteenth and nineteenth centuries, when literacy became possible for everyone, not just the privileged few, and toleration for differing religious points of view became more accepted. Naturally, a figure like Saint Nicholas in such an environment would be ecumenicized and the secular trend would continue. With the state taking over the role of caregiver to every citizen there was no longer the old reliance on God to take care of you, to sustain you, to rescue you. The result was even more secularization.

And the end result was Santa Claus. Still a good, kind figure, yes. In fact, a popular image as benign as one could get. And do we ever need such influences in

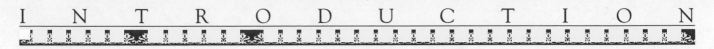

today's rootless society, awash in violence and sexuality divorced from love!

Looking back on my own life, I note that my conservative minister father, who dressed up in a Santa suit every Christmas, kept our Christmases spiritual, wedding the best of the spiritual and secular worlds. He recognized that we do have to coexist in both.

But Santa Claus alone—or even Saint Nicholas alone—without the life, crucifixion, death, and resurrection of our Lord is a travesty on what Christmas is all about! Christ *is* indeed, and must remain, the central core, the reason behind the season.

The Sixth Collection

"Now tell me, *surely* one of these *has* to be your personal favorite!"

Hundreds of times that question has been asked by people trying to decide which of the Christmas collections to buy first. And I tell them that's like asking which of my children I love most—I love each one for different reasons. Each has its own personality and idiosyncrasies.

So it is with this sixth collection. There are a number of unique things about it:

1. It concludes the Rosina Kiehlbauch Christmas in the Dakotas trilogy.

2. We bring back a number of the most beloved writers in our series—Hartley F. Dailey, Margaret E. Sangster, Jr., Pearl S. Buck, Bess Streeter Aldrich, and Terry Beck.

3. We are especially blessed by the authors represented in a *Christmas in My Heart* collection for the very first time—Arthur Gordon, Charles Sheldon, Lucy Maud Montgomery, Arthur Milward, Gary B. Swanson, Maimu Veedler, and Mae Hurley Ashworth.

4. I finally tackle the Saint Nicholas/Santa Claus story. (I've avoided it for five years, simply because it is so complex.)

5. For the first time, we are including several stories that bridge between Christmas and Hanukkah.

6. It includes a story I have wanted to write all my life—"Pandora's Books."

The write-in story of the year? Unquestionably, Pearl Buck's cherished story, "Matthew, Mark, Luke, and John."

Coda

I look forward to hearing from you! Please do keep the stories, responses, and suggestions coming. And not just for Christmas stories. I'm putting together collections centered around other genres as well. You may reach me by writing to:

Joe L. Wheeler, Ph.D.
c/o Review and Herald Publishing Association
55 West Oak Ridge Drive
Hagerstown, MD 21740

Small Things

Margaret E. Sangster, Jr.

Is anything ever really small in this life of ours? Or . . . might it be possible that some small things are, in reality, more significant than great things?

This great truth this virtually unknown Sangster story brings out, perhaps better than any other story I have ever known.

Margaret E. Sangster, Jr. [1894-1981], author of "The Littlest Orphan," "Lonely Tree," and "With a Star on Top," was one of the most beloved inspirational writers in America early in this century. Now, after teetering on the brink of oblivion for half a century, she is coming back. And we are all so much the richer for it!

Evie was trimming the Christmas tree. She was trimming it with tinsel and glass balls and imitation icicles. She was fastening a chubby small angel on the topmost branch when the doctor came in.

"Hello, darling," she called, peering down at him through a green barricade of branches (for the tree was tall, and Evie was standing on a little red ladder). "Hello, darling! Isn't this a swell angel!"

The doctor took off his fur-lined gloves and rubbed his hands together. He had been driving, and it was very cold, considerably colder than the usual December.

"No," he said, and his voice was as chill as the weather outside. "No, I don't like the angel. It's—It's too fat. It's obese. It looks like a kewpie."

Evie pouted. "I'm too fat myself," she said. "Christmas—and Christmas candy—has wrecked me, already. Maybe I look a trifle like a kewpie myself! And yet you like *me*."

"I'm engaged to you," said the doctor, "so it goes without saying that I like you."

"Usually, it does!" murmured Evie.

"And," the doctor continued, ignoring the interruption, "and you're grown up. You're not little. I hate little things."

"I'm not very tall," said Evie. Morosely, she began to clamber down the steps of the red ladder.

"That wasn't what I meant," said the doctor. "You're not tall, no. But you're an adult. That fool angel isn't. It looks like a baby I brought into the world this afternoon. An emergency Caesarean, it was. The mother was an Italian—it was her fifth child in five years. A nasty, fat, little wop baby."

Evie was all at once crouched down in front of the doctor. "Tell me about it," she begged. "Darling, tell me all about it. Just think, born on the afternoon before Christmas. What a break for a baby—"

The doctor snorted. "I'm not an obstetrician," he said. "It isn't my business, seeing that babies are born. On the afternoon before Christmas, or any afternoon. If all the other doctors in the world weren't off at strange places for the holidays I'd have told them to go to grass, to go somewhere else for their Caesarean. But there wasn't any alternative."

Evie's eyes were suddenly round in her round little face. "Don't you like babies, Ned? Or are you only having fun with me? Say you're only having fun! Because it—it isn't nice, this sort of pretend."

"Nice, my hat!" said the doctor. "I was the oldest of nine children. We were poor as mud. I saw my mother falter and fade and die under the burden of nine mouths to feed! Baby mouths—always open; always squalling! I worked for them, to keep them full, those mouths, when I was only a kid myself. Selling papers, printer's devil, running errands, everything. Snatched an education catch as catch can. I'd be a really great surgeon today, Evie, instead of a middling one, if I hadn't wasted so much time on the flock of them."

"Wasted?" queried Evie very softly.

"*Wasted!*" said the doctor savagely.

There was silence for a moment while snow beat with white insistent fingers against the window pane. While a fire danced on the hearth. While Evie tried, rather unsuccessfully, to braid her plump, small fingers.

"If we had babies, Ned," she asked softly, "you wouldn't mind it, would you? Keeping their little mouths full, I mean? You wouldn't even mind, would you, if there were nine of them? They couldn't *all* be babies at the same time!"

"There won't be nine of them," said the doctor. Curiously, his eyes watched Evie's fingers, lacing and unlacing. "There won't be any babies, Evie, not if I can help it! I've had babies enough in my life. I'm cured. I wish—" His tone was petulant; the emergency operation had been

a difficult one. "I wish that you'd keep your hands still. I've a headache, and it makes me nervous . . ."

Evie's fingers were strangely quiet for a moment. So, for that matter, was Evie. And then, with a sudden, swift movement the fingers were no longer quiet. The fingers of the right hand were very busy removing a ring—a ring that sparkled in the firelight from one of the fingers of the left hand.

"I'm afraid," said Evie, and it didn't sound like her voice, even to herself, "I'm afraid that I'll make you nervous, Ned, always and always. I'm"—she was dropping the ring into one of the doctor's hands— "I'm sorry."

The doctor hadn't been expecting the ring. It slipped between his fingers and lay on the rug, bright as a tear.

"For crying out loud!" said the doctor. "What are you getting at, Evie? Do you mean that you are—"

"I'm breaking our engagement!" answered Evie.

The doctor should have taken her into his arms and kissed her just then. He should have picked up the ring and forced it back upon the proper one of Evie's fingers. But he wasn't that sort. Instead he said stiffly, "I thought you loved me!"

"I thought I did," answered Evie. She was looking past him. "But I guess I don't. Not as much as I love babies . . . and fat, little angels . . . and other small things. . . ."

The doctor was rising swiftly. How was Evie to know that his head was all one throb and that the tears were very close to his eyes?

23

"Then it's goodbye?" he asked dully.

"It's goodbye!" agreed Evie.

She turned back to the tree and started, unsteadily, to mount the little red ladder.

The doctor drew on his fur-lined gloves, put on his great coat, and reached for his hat. He didn't speak again, neither did he stoop to retrieve the glimmering ring. He only walked out of Evie's living room, and out of Evie's apartment, and out of Evie's life. He only climbed into his waiting car and started, mechanically, to drive downtown through the blurring, blinding snow storm toward his own apartment. As he went along the great avenue he passed parks, each with its Christmas tree. They were like Evie's tree, magnified; and church yards, each with its tree, too. Over the door of one church hung a huge electric sign. It said "Good will toward men" in green and red lights. Seeing it, the doctor muttered something beneath his breath.

It was grim to be the afternoon before Christmas. As the doctor drove along the avenue he told himself that it was just the sort of a day on which to get unengaged. The snow looked gray instead of white, for it was very close to evening. The arc lights, already blazing, made shallow paths across its grayness. People hurrying to and fro were black, distorted shapes in the general gloom, like gnomes. There wasn't any shine to the eastern sky. There wasn't even the faintest hint of a star.

I'm dog tired, the doctor told himself, as he drove. *Maybe I'm asleep already and having a nightmare. This isn't happening to me!* (He loved Evie, you see, pretty, plump Evie. Very much indeed!) *It's happening,* he laughed painfully, *to a couple of other fellows.*

There wasn't any shine in the eastern sky. Even the light from the street lamps looked dirty. The doctor swung off the avenue and drove through the sedate brownstone-housed street on which he lived. He drew up in front of the old-fashioned, high-stooped place that was his home. It had been converted into apartments, that home. His apartment was on the ground floor.

"Thank God," he said wearily, "that I've no long flights of stairs to climb this night." And then, "I won't even take my car to the garage. It can stand in front until morning, and freeze."

Stiffly, he climbed out of the car. Achingly, he closed the car's door and locked it. And then, fumbling in his pocket for his keys, he mounted the steps of the high stoop. Perhaps it was the snow beating into his face that made him feel so suddenly blind. Perhaps it was something else. Perhaps . . .

The doctor uttered a sharp exclamation and paused. That dark blob on his doormat—he'd thought it was only a shadow, at first. He hadn't known until it cried that it was alive. He'd almost stepped on it! "For the love—" he began.

The blob upon the doormat lifted a furry black blot of a face and uttered a feeble complaint. It did more than lift its face; it lifted an infinitesimal black paw. The doctor saw that the paw was twisted oddly, unnaturally.

"A compound fracture at least," he heard himself saying, then felt foolish when he realized that the black blob was, after all, only a kitten.

A stray kitten, come to his doorstep from some grim, never-never land. A kitten that lifted its tiny, snow-drenched head and sobbed out its baby woe.

25

Sobbed out the agony and fear and lack of understanding that touches the soul of every homeless animal.

The doctor, his arms hanging limply at his sides, looked down at the forlorn little creature. "I should kick it off the porch," he said savagely. "Hateful, whining little beast." Suddenly all of his own agony and fear and lack of understanding were crystallized in the miserable bit of black fur. "You're the reason for it all!" he shouted down at the kitten. "You and—and things like you! If it weren't for you, I'd still be engaged. I'd—"

Gathering together all of its forces, the kitten struggled to three small feet. It limped piteously across the doormat. It crept agonizingly toward the doctor. It rubbed feebly against his trouser leg.

"Oh, no!" said the doctor. Stooping, he lifted the kitten into the curve of his arm. He held it gingerly, but even so he could tell that it was the thinnest kitten in the whole world. "Oh, goodness!" said the doctor. "Even a kitten's got a right to die indoors on the night before Christmas!"

After all, it *was* nearly dead! And it wasn't a human being either—it was only an animal. The doctor didn't know much about pets; he'd never had a pet, even when he was a boy. You see, he'd never really been a boy. But there was one thing that he did know, even when he was utterly spent, both of body and of soul. He knew surgery. He knew when a leg, even the leg of a worthless kitten, was all out of line. And he knew what should be done to make it assume proper proportions.

"If it were a horse," he said, as he unlocked the front door and crossed the general hall to unlock his apartment door, "if it were a horse I'd found on my doorstep"—the idea of a horse on his doorstep didn't seem remotely funny to the doctor at the time—"a horse with a broken leg, I'd call a policeman. And the policeman would come and shoot it and put it out of its misery! But"—the doctor switched on the lights in his living room—"one can't call a policeman to shoot a kitten."

It was as if the kitten understood. For blinking against the sudden flare of light, the kitten tucked his head into the hollow of the doctor's elbow and tried very feebly to purr.

"He's got guts, anyway," said the doctor. And then, all at once, the doctor reached for his handkerchief. "Oh, Evie!" said the doctor, and blew his nose violently. "Oh, Evie, *my dear* . . ."

The kitten snuggled closer. The purr was more feeble than it had been. Gingerly, the doctor ran his finger along the bone that rose aggressively high on the kitten's spine. "Probably," said the doctor, "he's dying now. But I'll get him some milk, anyway."

He carried the kitten carefully in the direction of his minute kitchenette. "After all, it's bad enough to die, but to die hungry . . ."

Oddly, the doctor found himself wondering whether, years from now, he himself would die hungry. *Heart hungry.*

There was milk in the kitchenette. The maid who came mornings to tidy up had forgotten to put it in the refrigerator, and for once the doctor was grateful for her carelessness. The milk wouldn't be clammy; it wouldn't be necessary to heat it. Still holding the kitten, he poured some of the milk, clumsily, into a cereal dish. Still holding the kitten, he thrust the dish under its nose.

"Drink that!" he commanded harshly. "You little pest!"

The kitten nuzzled its nose down into the saucer of milk. The doctor could feel the quiver of its desperate eagerness. Once, when he was an intern, he had treated a starvation case. He knew the symptoms.

"Slowly, there," he said to the kitten. "Don't go so fast." He held the saucer away for a moment, waiting until the kitten breathed more normally, then held it back again under the quivering nose. After a while the kitten drank more quietly, and under its drying fur the doctor could feel its little sides growing puffy. When finally the saucer was empty, it raised a small face, very daubed with milk. It looked very babyish for a moment. And then with a supreme effort, it lifted its well paw and began weakly to wash the milk from its face.

It was the effort back of that instinctive cleaning that decided the doctor—decided him, for better or for worse.

"A gentleman like you," said the doctor, "deserves two paws to wash with."

With something like respect in the line of his mouth, in the expression of his eyes, he carried the sated kitten back to the living room. There was a broad mahogany table in the living room that held books and copies of the A.M.A. *Journal* and Evie's picture in a white jade frame. The doctor removed the books and the magazines and put a flat cushion from one of the chairs in their place. But Evie's picture he didn't move.

"Maybe," he said to the picture, "you'd like me better if you could see me do something I'm really good at!"

He laid the kitten on the cushion and went into the bathroom for his emergency kit and some towels. The doctor had his office in a hospital; he hadn't much equipment at home. But he had enough, quite enough, to take care of the needs of a kitten.

Gently carrying his emergency case, he came back to the living room and his patient. The patient was drowsing from the triple result of food, warmth, and pain. With fingers surprisingly tender—for they were very large—he took the kitten's injured paw in his hand and parted the fur. The kitten stirred and whimpered, but he didn't scratch. The kitten seemed to *know*.

"Whew!" said the doctor, surveying the paw. It wasn't only broken, it was mangled. It looked as if it had been chewed. It might have been.

"Amputation," said the doctor.

There was ether in the emergency case. The doctor went into the bathroom again for cotton and a medicine dropper. On the way back he had a thought. "Why not put it to sleep?" he asked himself. "Permanently. Life's hard enough for whole things, let alone maimed."

But then he met Evie's pictured eyes, smiling at him from out of their chaste white jade frame. And at almost the same moment he remembered how the kitten had washed its face with one paw.

"I'll show you, honey," he found himself saying wildly to the picture (he'd never called Evie anything like that to her face). "And I won't amputate, either! *It can be done!*"

Little by little, with the aid of the cotton and the medicine dropper, the doctor put the little kitten to sleep. It lay very limp and soft under his hand. Its fur had dried longer than most kitten fur, and fluffier. And then, very tenderly, much more tenderly than he had worked the week before upon the shin bone of a multimillionaire, he began to operate. Upon a thing so tiny that it might have been a smudge of ink, so broken that God Himself, who watches over sparrows, must have known pity.

It wasn't an easy operation. It took a long while. Once, briefly, the doctor looked up from his task and sighed as he met Evie's watchful gaze. "The patient was on the operating table for a matter of hours," he said. It was the closest the doctor had ever come to being whimsical.

And then, at last, the operation was over, and the sad little paw was miraculously fitted together into some semblance of proper mechanics, held together with splints. (Made of those wooden things that physicians put upon your tongue when they ask you to say "Ahh.") And over the splints was wound a white, firm, tidy bandage that looked extremely professional. And smelled so, too.

"And that," said the doctor, "is that!"

The kitten stirred, ever so slightly, but it wasn't ready yet to come out of the ether. It had had quite a lot of ether for a kitten. The doctor, seeing it move, looked at his wrist watch. The kitten's movement had been very sleepy.

"My word!" he said, for it was very late, indeed. *"My word!"*

No use now to think about dinner. The restaurant down the street, where he so often ate when he was alone, would be closed. But there was still milk in the kitchenette, and probably bread, too. Bread and milk was good enough for anyone.

But as he was eating the bread and milk out of a deep bowl, the doctor was remembering a telephone conversation he'd had that morning with Evie.

"We'll have our dinner at my place tonight," she had said. "I am, believe it or not, going to cook it. It will be a goose."

The doctor wondered whether Evie was eating her goose alone.

"You can't have your goose and eat it too!" he found himself saying, and wondered seriously if he had gone mad. Perhaps he had. Perhaps this major operation which he had just performed on such a minor part of life was only one of the delusions that went with madness. Just to make himself feel sane he ate a second bowl of bread and milk, although he didn't really want it. That didn't make him feel sane, either. Just stuffy.

And the kitten wasn't a delusion. For as the doctor left the kitchenette and wended his way toward the living room, he heard sounds from the kitten. Sounds of utter, racking distress.

"How could I have been such a fool!" the doctor questioned as he broke into a trot. "All that ether on top of all that milk! *No wonder!"*

For the kitten was being violently, dreadfully sick at its tummy. It had come out of the ether and had started all over again to taste the bitterness of existence. It raised sad eyes in a peaked black face to the man who had tried so hard to save its life. And then its eyes rolled back strangely and a convulsive shudder took its little body into a dreadful, wrenching paroxysm.

The doctor stood beside the table looking down,

dazedly, at the kitten. For a moment he stood there, and then he was galvanized into action. He picked the little thing up swiftly in his clever hands and was forcing open the tiny, rigid mouth.

"Oh, no, you don't!" he said, and his voice was half a sob. "Oh, no, you won't! Not *now*. I won't let you die. Not after bringing you through the hardest operation I've ever done!"

The rigid little mouth was open now. Into it the doctor was dropping a brown liquid. Not much, just a little, from a slim vial in his emergency box. The tremors in the little body began to pass. Two kitten eyes rolled back to normal. And the doctor found that he was wiping beads of sweat from his own forehead.

"You—*kitten!*" he said softly. "Don't you let me catch you acting up again! Don't you dare . . ." His voice broke on a high note.

But the little kitten . . . Oh, it wasn't that the little kitten didn't want to mind. Only he'd had rather a bad time of it. Cold, privation, hunger, racking agony, anesthetics . . . He'd hardly been old enough to know so many sensations, really!

All through the night, the night before Christmas, the doctor fought for a little kitten's life, a life that hung by a black little thread. Fought for that—and for something else. Fought for the rebirth of love in the pictured eyes of a girl. Fought for a rebirth of tenderness. He fought with patient, prayerful hands, and with slim, sharp instruments. He fought with hot compresses and ice packs. He fought, toward dawn, with a stimulant and hot milk. He didn't know that the room was chill with the chill that comes before sunup. He didn't know

that it had stopped snowing. He didn't know, even, that it was Christmas day. He only knew when a tired little kitten thrust out a wee, pinkish tongue to lick his fingers that he had won a victory out of all proportion to the life of a small animal.

"Well," he said, as the kitten's rough tongue touched his hand, "you've got eight lives left. As I see it, you should devote 'em all to catching mice—for me."

Wearily, he threw himself down in one of the wide soft chairs that were his greatest luxury. But when the kitten cried softly because it felt abandoned, he got up again. And taking the tiny thing softly into his arms, he went back to the chair.

The kitten snuggled up against his chest, yawning, in a languorous moment of peace after the storm. The doctor yawned, too.

When the maid, who came mornings to tidy up, entered the living room, they were still in the chair, sleeping—a man with a curious pallor on his still face, and a mere scrap of a kitten with a front paw in splints and bandages.

The maid, being by this time immune to the oddity of physicians, tiptoed through the living room and toward the kitchen. She made coffee and toast. She pushed the coffee pot to the back of the stove and ate the toast herself.

It was ten o'clock, perhaps, when she tiptoed through the living room again to answer the buzz of the front doorbell. She opened the door with her finger to her lips.

A girl stood there. A pretty, rather plump girl in a fur coat. A girl with trembling lips and dark circles under her eyes.

"I want to see Ned," the girl began. "The doctor," she corrected herself primly.

The maid recognized the girl. She'd dusted the frame around her picture every day for months. But she was a glum maid; she didn't smile.

"The doctor's asleep," she said. "Can I take a message?"

The girl spoke with a rush. "I'm not a patient," she said. "I am—I was—a friend of the doctor's. He—he dropped something yesterday in my house. I—I found it on the floor after he'd gone. It's something valuable. I wanted to return it to him."

The maid relaxed. She almost achieved a pleasant expression. "You can wait," she said, "I guess." With a jerk of her hand, she indicated a figure in a great chair, a figure seen on a slant through an inner doorway. "He can't sleep *much* longer!"

The girl stepped into the apartment and closed the door after her. She wasn't a stranger to the place; she'd been there before. She went straight through the inner doorway into the living room—and paused before the miracle of that room. The miracle of a table littered with cotton and bandages and medicine droppers and teaspoons and saucers of clotting milk. And at the calm among the litter—a girl's portrait in a frame of white jade. The miracle of a chair with an exhausted man sprawled in it, a man with a smudge of dust on one cheek, and a slight film of beard (such as most men have before shaving time), and his collar wrenched open at the throat. And threads of lint from torn bandages clinging to his trousers. Of a man sleeping dreamlessly, sleeping with a wee morsel of a black kitten curled up on his chest. *Almost* curled, for one paw was held out stiffly in splints.

The man didn't awaken as Evie crossed the room on light, incredulous feet. But the black kitten's eyes came suddenly open. Its pink mouth came open, too, in a yawn. The yawn turned into a tiny yap of pain as the kitten tried to stretch. Stretching wouldn't be easy for quite a few days.

Evie looked at the kitten. She looked at the sleeping man. And then, all at once, her round little face was glorified, and her eyes were as tender as Mary's eyes must have been on the very first Christmas Day of all.

Very quietly she opened the purse that she carried. It was a frivolous blue purse with a tassel. She took something from it, something that glimmered like the kind of a tear that grows out of extreme happiness. She slipped that something upon the third finger of her left hand.

And then she sat down in a chair, very quietly, to wait.

She was so quiet, in fact, that the small kitten yawned again and went back to sleep.

The Servant Candle

Terry Beck

One of the most beautiful and meaningful developments during the last generation or so is the trend in Christian churches to honor, remember, and, in many cases, observe a number of Jewish customs and traditions, recognizing that the traditions which our Lord Himself honored and observed while on earth are ours as well.

Terry Beck, author of one of the most treasured Christmas in My Heart *stories, "The Jubilee Agreement," is the mother of six children and today lives in Mount Hermon, California. She was raised in a Jewish home, but later, after reading the New Testament in a philosophy class, became a Christian. Today she feels blessed by this intermingling of Jewish and Christian traditions.*

For those of us who know little of the impact of Hanukkah on family life, this story cannot help but warm the heart.

W e're home." Ruth Cohen Starr whispered to the infant propped against her shoulder. She leaned her head wearily against the airplane window. *What a ragtag team we are, widowed and fatherless.*

Whining engines picked up the chant she'd repeated ever since Daniel's funeral: *What am I to do now, God? What am I going to do now?*

"Life goes on, Ruth," a neighbor commented before her departure. "And there will be meaning and joy again. For now, just do the next thing. Love your baby. In time, God will heal your wounds."

Unfastening her seat belt, waiting to disembark, Ruth stared at the nameplate on her worn travel bag: Ruth Althea Cohen, Beloved Healer of Sorrows. Names were important to the Cohens. When Ruth was young, Grandpa Asa explained that the children of Abraham and Sarah Cohen were named alphabetically, by prayers.

Ruth sighed. Her parents' death, when she was 10, left her feeling abandoned. Now she felt abandoned again. *"Healer of Sorrows"* was a misnomer, she thought ruefully. *"Bearer of Sorrows" would be more accurate.*

Her brow furrowed with attempted optimism. Hanukkah was coming. Ruth pitied non-Jewish friends who missed this celebration. Unsure how her own Jewish family came to claim Jesus as the Messiah, Ruth did know their faith was beautifully expressed through the old Jewish and new Christian traditions.

This Hanukkah promised to be unique. Sofia, an honorary aunt to the Cohen family, requested everyone's presence. *Why?* Ruth wondered. She plucked Isaac off the seat, suddenly feeling too drained to think about such mysteries. It was enough to do the next thing. She smiled bravely for her family waiting with open arms in the terminal.

* * *

31

Back in her childhood setting, old friends dropped by to share their lives, many full of struggles. Ruth listened with new awareness and compassion. Had youth and naiveté hidden this pain? Had widowhood initiated her into a sorority of wounded hearts she'd formerly ignored?

Facing these mid-December days became easier as Ruth pushed away her own grief to encourage others. She began to look forward to using her own experience to cheer those who had come to bolster her.

The first night of Hanukkah, Asa retold the story of the Maccabees' victory over the Romans. The final night's celebration included the savored dinner of *kreplach* (Jewish ravioli with cheese filling) and *latkes* (potato pancakes) with applesauce; then the candle-lighting service in Aunt Dara's darkened living room. Ruth prepared for the Time of Honor, sitting in the circle of chairs with her family.

Grandpa Asa opened the ceremonies. "It is my privilege on this eighth night of Hanukkah to light the first candle on our menorah," he said. "We honor Aunt Sofia who has blessed us over many years. Sofia, a refugee from the war, who joined us after our parents died—an angel sent by God to distract us from our grief. I, Asa Eleazar Cohen, light the first candle for Sofia, who arrived tiny and frail, but with an inner strength we did not understand. She put aside her own anguish to bring us into the Kingdom of God."

Where did her strength come from? Ruth wondered.

Aunt Bettina, an auburn-haired beauty, interrupted these thoughts. Moving to the menorah, Bettina began: "When Simon was in the Navy, our cabin on Guam was isolated. I was enormously pregnant, and Simon was at sea when a typhoon hit. The winds were maniacal. In haste to fasten the storm shutters, I slipped, landing hard. A shutter fell across my belly and see-sawed over me. I wept helplessly as rain battered me into the mud. Then black boots approached and an umbrella blocked the rain. A soft hand stroked my cheek. Aunt Sofia half-carried me inside to a hot bath, and then fastened the shutters. We sat out that typhoon by candlelight, Sophia calming my fears. I asked her the source of her strength. 'Jesus,' she said and told me about the Messiah who had come. I accepted Christ's gift. Five days later, Nathan, God's gift to me, was born. Now I, Bettina Ann Cohen Aaron, light this candle in honor of Aunt Sofia, whose miraculous presence brought me new life."

New life, Ruth thought. *Oh, how good it would be to start over!*

Uncle Chaim stood. "In college, Pearl and I wanted to marry," he said, "but we had no place to live. Sofia took a shovel and dug out a room in the basement, then paid carpenters to finish the work! We married immediately. I, Chaim Alexander Cohen, light this candle for Sofia, who lovingly labored for the sake of our happiness."

Ruth shifted sleeping Isaac from one arm to another. She listened to Dara's, Franz's, and Gabriella's stories and glanced at Sophia. Laugh lines ran from eyes that seemed to know forever.

Then big, redheaded Eli brandished the *shammash*, stirring a breeze that threatened the flames. Ruth studied the menorah as Eli dedicated his candle.

"The first time I fell in love," he chuckled, "was with a motorcycle. Chaim forbade it, but this wild rebel bought a Harley. I wiped out immediately, breaking both

legs. Sofia's chicken soup healed them as her bedside conversation healed my soul. I, Elijah Zebulon Cohen, light this candle for Sofia, the best nurse in the world."

Herschel's rebel smile made Ruth smile as he stood and patted his pony-tail teasingly. "As an angry teenager I moved to a commune," he said, sobering. "I intended to abandon family forever. After several lonely months, I was summoned to the visiting room. Sofia had come. We walked in the garden, and I learned her story.

"At 19 she married Thom, a Gentile. Her parents disowned her. War came. Being married to a Jew became illegal. Thom took their two daughters to Warsaw for safety. Sofia was deported. The war ended after much horror. For three years Sofia searched for her family. They had vanished. Relocation officials told Sofia she could go to America, if she found a sponsor. Sofia knew no one here, but the Cohen children agreed to sponsor anyone from the war who was looking for a family. Sofia came to us."

Sophia brushed away a tear, then a wisp of hair, to hide her emotion, as Herschel told how he talked a long time with Sophia.

"Then she stopped me," he said, "and told me, 'A family can be a burden, but only a miracle can heal the despair of losing one forever.'" Herschel's voice broke. "I, Herschel Lazarus Cohen, light this candle in honor of Sofia, who reached a confused kid and renewed the love that brought me home."

Ruth wiped her eyes on Isaac's burp cloth. Fragments of these stories were familiar, but she had never known Sofia's role in them. She watched Sofia

CIMH6-3

rise quietly and move into the light, white hair crowning a serene face.

"Important things you must understand," Sofia said firmly. "On the boat to America another refugee traveled with me. She also survived the horrors, but where I despaired, she rejoiced. I asked how joy was possible. 'Messiah Jesus knows all pain,' she said, and told me His story. I accepted Jesus. There was much I didn't understand. What was God calling me to do? How would I fit into the gracious, Jewish Cohen family, now that I would follow Christ?"

Asa *did* cringe, Sophia remembered, when she explained her new faith. But he suggested she try Cohen family life. With nowhere to go, no other vision, Sophia agreed.

The first Hanukkah with the Cohens answered many questions. Each of Sarah and Abraham Cohen's children lit a candle during the Time of Honor. Eight candles, eight children. Little Herschel worried about a candle for Sophia to light. He studied the menorah.

"Aunt Sofia," he said, "you can light the *shammash,* the servant candle that lights all the others. The *shammash* is important. The other candles can only be lit with it."

"Through Herschel's words," Sophia said, "God offered me a vision for rebuilding my life. A servant candle wouldn't shine in memorial to ancient struggles or be watched breathlessly until it burned out. It must light other candles to proclaim faith, hope, and victory. And this was the meaning of Hanukkah—dedication. This would be my life's dedication, to be a *shammash.*"

Sofia paused, pulling wrinkled papers from her pocket. For a long minute she stared. "This letter is from my daughter, Annya," she whispered. "Forgive me." She choked on the words, weeping openly. "You must imagine what this means, to hear from one long thought dead! Annya survived typhus; my other child did not. Now Annya and her husband teach in Romania. Their baby has AIDS. They need a *shammash.* I must go to care for my granddaughter."

Sofia set her candle in the menorah. "I, Sofia Azelina Kotlowitz, pray your words tonight indicate I've been a worthy *shammash,*" she said, "and have returned a portion of the joy and purpose you've given me. I pray you'll light the flame of those you love. Help them to be a light to others. I will not again light your servant candle."

Gently she blew out the flame.

"Kindling your *shammash* has been the blessing and redemption of my life," she said. "But now one of you will be called as the Cohen *shammash* to offer the Messiah's illumination and comfort here."

"You are worthy of honor, Sofia!" came a voice from the middle of the room.

"Yes," chimed the others, "you are worthy."

Isaac's drowsy form held Ruth in place as the clan

engulfed Sofia. Her soul stirred as if awakened from a deep slumber.

Grandpa Asa broke away from the group. "You OK, Ruthie?" he asked.

Ruth nodded slowly.

"Sofia Azelina means 'wise one spared by God,'" he observed. "Suffering refines the heart, Ruth. We believe you may have a calling before you."

"What do you mean, Grandpa?" Ruth asked.

"We believe God may be calling you to be the next *shammash* for us," Asa whispered. "He calls one whose ministry needs focus and vision, whose life offers strength and compassion. The *shammash* reflects the Light of the world. Think about it, Ruth Althea, our beloved healer of sorrows. Listen. God is speaking."

"I am listening, Grandpa," Ruth whispered, resting a wet cheek on his gnarled hand. "For the first time since Daniel's death I am hearing God's voice loud and clear." She stood, shifting Isaac to her shoulder, drawn irresistibly to Sophia.

There was much she wanted to learn before the gift of the servant candle passed to her hands.

Clorinda's Gifts

Lucy Maud Montgomery

"It is a dreadful thing to be poor a fortnight before Christmas," said Clorinda to Aunt Emmy. Clorinda didn't see how she could possibly give away gifts at all, but Aunt Emmy kept coming back to a line from a famous poem: "The gift without the giver is bare."

It took four days, but Clorinda did figure it out.

Lucy Maud Montgomery (1874-1942), author of Anne of Green Gables, *and Canada's most famous author, was also a splendid writer of short stories, as this story reveals.*

I t is a dreadful thing to be poor a fortnight before Christmas," said Clorinda with the mournful sigh of 17 years.

Aunt Emmy smiled. Aunt Emmy was 60 and spent the hours she didn't spend in a bed on a sofa or in a wheel chair; but Aunt Emmy was never heard to sigh. "I suppose it is worse then than at any other time," she admitted.

That was one of the nice things about Aunt Emmy. She always sympathized and understood.

"I'm worse than poor this Christmas—I'm stony broke," said Clorinda dolefully. "My spell of fever in the summer and the consequent doctor's bills have cleaned out my coffers completely. Not a single Christmas present can I give. And I did so want to give some little thing to each of my dearest people. But I simply can't afford it; that's the hateful, ugly truth." Clorinda sighed again.

"The gifts which money can purchase are not the only ones we can give," said Aunt Emmy gently. "Nor the best, either."

"Oh, I know it's nicer to give something of your own work," agreed Clorinda, "but materials for fancy work cost, too. That kind of gift is just as much out of the question for me as any other."

"That was not what I meant," said Aunt Emmy.

"What did you mean, then?" asked Clorinda, looking puzzled.

Aunt Emmy smiled. "Suppose you think out my meaning for yourself," she said. "That would be better than if I explained it. Besides, I don't think I *could* explain it. Take the beautiful line of a beautiful poem to help you in your thinking out: 'The gift without the giver is bare.'"

"I'd put it the other way and say, 'The giver without the gift is bare,'" said Clorinda, with a grimace. "That is my predicament exactly. Well, I hope by next Christmas I'll not be quite so bankrupt. I'm going into Mr. Callender's store down at Murraybridge in February. He has offered me the place, you know."

"Won't your aunt miss you terribly?" asked Aunt Emmy gravely.

Clorinda flushed. There was a note in Aunt Emmy's voice that disturbed her. "Oh, yes, I suppose she will," she answered hurriedly. "But she'll get used to it very soon. And I will be home every Saturday night, you know. I'm dreadfully tired of being poor, Aunt Emmy, and now that I have a chance to earn something for my-

self I mean to take it. I can help Aunt Mary, too. I'm to get $4 a week."

"I think she would rather have your companionship than a part of your salary, Clorinda," said Aunt Emmy. "But, of course, you must decide for yourself, dear. It is hard to be poor. I know it; I am poor."

"You poor!" said Clorinda, kissing her. "Why, you are the richest woman I know, Aunt Emmy—rich in love and goodness and contentment."

"And so are you, dearie—rich in youth and health and happiness and ambition. Aren't they all worthwhile?"

"Of course, they are," laughed Clorinda. "Only, unfortunately, Christmas gifts can't be coined out of them."

"Did you ever try?" asked Aunt Emmy. "Think out that question, too, in your thinking out, Clorinda."

"Well, I must say bye-bye and run home. I feel cheered up; you always cheer people up, Aunt Emmy. How gray it is outdoors. I do hope we'll have snow soon. Wouldn't it be jolly to have a white Christmas? We always have such faded brown Decembers."

Clorinda lived just across the road from Aunt Emmy in a tiny white house behind some huge willows. But Aunt Mary lived there, too, the only relative Clorinda had, for Aunt Emmy wasn't really her aunt at all. Clorinda had always lived with Aunt Mary, ever since she could remember.

Clorinda went home and upstairs to her little room under the eaves, where the great bare willow boughs were branching athwart her windows. She was thinking over what Aunt Emmy had said about Christmas gifts and giving.

"I'm sure I don't know what she could have

meant," pondered Clorinda. "I do wish I could find out, if it would help me any. I'd love to remember a few of my friends at least. There's Miss Mitchell . . . She's been so good to me all this year and helped me so much with my studies. And there's Mrs. Martin out in Manitoba. If I could only send her something! She must be so lonely out there. And Aunt Emmy herself, of course; and poor old Aunt Kitty down the lane; and Aunt Mary and yes—Florence, too, although she did treat me so meanly. I shall never feel the same to her again. But she gave me a present last Christmas, and so out of mere politeness I ought to give her something."

Clorinda stopped short suddenly. She had just remembered that she would not have liked to say that last sentence to Aunt Emmy. Therefore, there was something wrong about it. Clorinda had long ago learned that there was sure to be something wrong in anything that could not be said to Aunt Emmy. So she stopped to think it over.

Clorinda puzzled over Aunt Emmy's meaning for four days and part of three nights. Then all at once it came to her. Or if it wasn't Aunt Emmy's meaning it was a very good meaning in itself, and it grew clearer and expanded in meaning during the days that followed, although at first Clorinda shrank a little from some of the conclusions to which it led her.

"I've solved the problem of my Christmas giving for this year," she told Aunt Emmy. "I have some things to give after all. Some of them quite costly, too. That is, they will cost me something, but I know I'll be better off and richer after I've paid the price. That is what Mr.

Grierson would call a paradox, isn't it? I'll explain all about it to you on Christmas Day."

On Christmas Day Clorinda went over to Aunt Emmy's. It was a faded brown Christmas after all, for the snow had not come. But Clorinda did not mind; there was such joy in her heart that she thought it the most delightful Christmas Day that ever dawned.

She put the strange-looking armful she carried down on the kitchen floor before she went into the sitting room. Aunt Emmy was lying on the sofa before the fire, and Clorinda sat down beside her.

"I've come to tell you all about it," she said.

Aunt Emmy patted the hand that was in her own. "From your face, dear girl, it will be pleasant hearing and telling," she said.

Clorinda nodded. "Aunt Emmy, I thought for days over your meaning—thought until I was dizzy. And then one evening it just came to me, without any thinking at all, and I knew that I could give some gifts after all. I thought of something new every day for a week. At first, I didn't think I *could* give some of them, and then I thought how selfish I was. I would have been willing to pay any amount of money for gifts if I had had it, but I wasn't willing to pay what I had. I got over that, though, Aunt Emmy. Now I'm going to tell you what I *did* give.

"First, there was my teacher, Miss Mitchell. I gave her one of Father's books. I have so many of his, you know, so that I wouldn't miss one; but still it was one I loved very much, and so I felt that that love made it worthwhile. That is, I felt that on second thought. At first, Aunt Emmy, I thought I would be ashamed to offer Miss Mitchell a shabby old book, worn with much reading and all marked over with Father's notes and pencillings. I was afraid she would think it queer of me to give her such a present. And yet, somehow it seemed to me that it was better than something brand new and unmellowed—that old book Father had loved and that I loved. So I gave it to her, and she understood. I think it pleased her so much, the real meaning in it. She said it was like being given something out of another's heart and life.

"Then you know Mrs. Martin. Last year she was Miss Hope, my dear Sunday school teacher. She married a home missionary, and they are in a lonely part of the West. Well, I wrote her a letter. Not just an ordinary letter; dear me, no! I took a whole day to write it, and you should have seen the postmistress' eyes stick out when I mailed it. I just told her everything that had happened in Greenvale since she went away. I made it as newsy and cheerful and loving as I possibly could. Everything bright and funny I could think of went into it.

"The next was old Aunt Kitty. You know she was my nurse when I was a baby, and she's very fond of me. But, well, you know, Aunt Emmy, I'm ashamed to confess it, but really I've never found Aunt Kitty very entertaining, to put it mildly. She is always glad when I go to see her, but I've never gone except when I couldn't help it. She is very deaf, and rather dull and stupid, you know. Well, I gave her a whole day. I took my knitting yesterday and sat with her the whole time and just talked and talked. I told her all the Greenvale news and gossip and everything else I thought she'd like to hear. She was so pleased and proud; she told me when I came

away that she hadn't had such a nice time for years.

"Then there was . . . Florence. You know, Aunt Emmy, we were always intimate friends until last year. Then Florence once told Rose Watson something I had told her in confidence. I found it out and I was so hurt. I couldn't forgive Florence, and I told her plainly I could never be a real friend to her again. Florence felt badly, because she really did love me, and she asked me to forgive her, but it seemed as if I couldn't. Well, Aunt Emmy, that was my Christmas gift to her—my forgiveness. I went down last night and just put my arms around her and told her that I loved her as much as ever and wanted to be real close friends again.

"I gave Aunt Mary her gift this morning. I told her I wasn't going to Murraybridge, that I just meant to stay home with her. She was so glad—and I'm glad, too, now that I've decided so."

"Your gifts have been real gifts, Clorinda," said Aunt Emmy. "Something of you—the best of you—went into each of them."

Clorinda went out and brought her bulky armful in. "I didn't forget you, Aunt Emmy," she said, as she unpinned the paper.

There was a rosebush—Clorinda's own pet rosebush—all snowed over with fragrant blossoms.

Aunt Emmy loved flowers. She put her finger under one of the roses and kissed it. "It's as sweet as yourself, dear child," she said tenderly. "And it will be a joy to me all through the lonely winter days. You've found out the best meaning of Christmas giving, haven't you, dear?"

"Yes, thanks to you, Aunt Emmy," said Clorinda softly.

So Cold, So Far From Home

Maimu Veedler

Some time ago I received a letter with a Canadian post-mark. Maimu Veedler of Lively, Ontario, had been instrumental in discovering Cathy Miller's memorable story, "Delayed Delivery," which was published in Christmas in My Heart, *book 2. This was a long letter, a moving letter; so much so that I wrote her asking for further information. She answered that the fuller story of her ordeal is told by Lilya Vinglas Wagner in* To Linger Is to Die, *edited by Gerald Wheeler and published by Southern Publishing Association, Nashville, in 1975.*

With her blessing, I have edited Mrs. Veedler's hand-written story, but it needed very few substantive changes. Reading it, perhaps, will remind us all just how much we have to be thankful for.

Christmas! That beautiful magical time of the year. It always, always comes around once a year. Nothing can stop it or delay it. Not even wars. Sometimes wracked with pain, yes. Sometimes suppressed, yes. Sometimes deprived of it altogether, yes. But stop it? *Never!*

It sometimes seems unreal to me that I am now old and can watch my children and grandchildren grow up in a land blessed with freedom and abundance and, perhaps most meaningful of all, being free to enjoy Christmas to the utmost.

It was not so a little more than a half century ago. The year was 1944, and war was raging across Europe. My friends and I had just entered our magical late teens with all our beautiful dreams ahead of us. The war robbed us of all those dreams; robbed us too of our happy homes, loving parents, and even our beloved homeland, forcing us to flee as empty-handed refugees to a strange land and language, where we were neither wanted nor welcomed.

Though it was autumn, the war was not yet over. The Germans were retreating, but the bombing never stopped. So many young men had died that the girls were forced to put on uniforms and operate ammunition factories, defense systems, and army field hospitals. From my forlorn little country of Estonia the lucky ones had escaped over the Baltic Sea to Sweden. Less lucky ones were often torpedoed while trying to escape by ship. The *really* unlucky ones had to stay and succumb to the horrors of the Russian invasion.

In the lands controlled by the Third Reich, the young single girls were rounded up and forcibly sent to army boot camps, fitted with the same coarse uniforms men wore, and then shipped out to wherever they were needed most.

Since we had lost all contact with our families, almost desperately we tried to remain together with our friends from home.

December came, and we found ourselves in a bleak

army boot camp in Punitz, east of Berlin, together with hundreds of girls sent there from all over German-occupied Europe. We were first fumigated, fitted with men's Luftwaffe uniforms, and separated (according to nationalities) into barracks, 30 girls to each room. We Estonians filled two rooms, and were awaiting transport to a nurses' training camp in Austria.

And the second snow came. It was bitterly cold. In each room, there was only one small iron stove; but even worse, we were only allowed a few bricks of coal a day. In order to avoid freezing, we got creative. Each of our bunk beds had straw mattresses and was supported by 10 wooden slats; we decided to see if we could make it on five. The "surplus" slats we secretly used as firewood. When we had used up all those in the bottom bunks, we started on the upper bunks, and that's when trouble began. When a top bunk sleeper proved to be restless, we would all awaken to hear that person crashing through upon the poor unfortunate person below, who was already reduced to half of *her* slats! It seems funny now, but it was not very funny then.

Our large, frigid room was divided by rows of narrow metal lockers. Behind them were our bunks. In the front was the lone stove, a large table, and a chair for each of us. Among the 30 girls sitting around the table, all sleeping in the same room, all marching together, there was no distinction as to who was rich and who was poor. Nothing that our parents had had counted now, for all was lost. Some of the girls had attended school with me, had been brought up with maids and given anything that money would buy. And some of the girls had been too poor to secure an education, so had

41

to hire out as maids. But now we were all just one big family, hanging on to each other for dear life, known only by our personality and character.

Our thin-walled washrooms at the edge of the compound were even worse. The water was ice-cold; there was even snow in the corners. Every morning our standard routine was to dash into the washroom, scrub ourselves from head to toe, dress in record time, and race out. Then came the daily routine: training, lectures, potato peeling, and coal lugging.

We all came from a culture where Christmas started at sundown on Christmas Eve. Traditional were ginger cookies, sausages, sauerkraut, and sweet coffee bread. The fresh fir tree would be brought into the house early Christmas morning and decorated with wax candles, cookies, candies, and apples (these were all treats for the children). Only rich people exchanged presents. When it got dark, most people went to their churches for Christmas services, then returned home to eat, light the candles, and sing our traditional carols. It was a joyous time, a family time, filled with the peace and contentment the Christ-filled season always brought. In the following days we visited friends and family.

What a contrast all that was to our bitterly cold barracks! On the morning of December 24, we were read the "riot act." No one was permitted to trespass the privately-owned woods just outside the camp. Anyone caught cutting even the tiniest of fir trees would be severely punished. Each room full of girls was "graciously" allowed one branch of a fir tree as decoration—if it was asked for. And that had to come from the camp property. Next, 10 of the girls from our room were sent to haul the coal; I

was one of them. When we had loaded the truck, we all had to climb up and sit on top of the coal heap. As we traveled back to camp, it was just awful to be sitting on this whole truckload of coal, and yet know that we'd end up with only a few bricks for our little stove.

Well, I decided to do something about it (the German army men would have called what I did "organizing," rather than "stealing"). I filled my army pantlegs with a goodly number of coal bricks. This worked fine while I was sitting down, but just try walking that way! And since the German soldiers were watching us as we got off the truck, there was no chance to transfer the bricks. The girls (bless them) saved me; we all chattered in Estonian, which the soldiers didn't understand, fortunately, and as it was so terribly cold, the soldiers didn't think it was strange that we were all huddled together, with me in the center, as we returned to our barracks. Once there, we hastily hid the bricks in our mattresses. Ah! For once we were going to be warm that night!

We were hungry, but not starving. After all, the German men had precious little to eat, themselves; but somehow we got fed enough to survive on. That Christmas Eve we gathered around our bleak empty table with its one lone candle in the middle. But we did have a tiny Christmas "tree" on top of the lockers. Well, there we were, singing our beloved carols and struggling to hold back the tears, when in marched the *Fuhrerin* for her nightly roll call. As her sharp eyes caught sight of our tiny tree, her face distorted in fury, and she barked out our punishment. Then one of the girls pushed apart the lockers and brought the tree to the *Fuhrerin*. Suddenly speechless, she gave us a murderous look and stormed out of our room. The tiny "tree" was just our allotted branch, cut into pieces, and tied with red wool to the top of a broom handle, then stuck between two lockers so it would stay vertical!

In the shock of her hateful look and slammed door, there was a long silence. Then each of the 30 faces began to lose the fearful look, lips began to twitch and then laugh until it hurt. After some time passed, we again sang a carol or two. But what *next?* It was still Christmas Eve and far too early to go to bed.

Someone said, "I wish we could have the 'Christmas Evangelicum.'"

But nobody had smuggled in a Bible. Nobody but me.

So the mood lifted again. We had a Bible, so we could hear the Christmas story after all! So I opened my Bible to the Gospel of Saint Matthew. That's where I thought the Christmas story *should* have been. But it was not! I knew I could recite the story from memory, but they wanted it *read!* So I hastily leaped into Saint Mark—and couldn't find it there, either. By now I was starting to panic. I tried Saint Luke next. (If that failed, there was still Saint John left.)

Suddenly, *there it was!* The second chapter.

"And it came to pass in those days, that there went out a decree from Caesar Augustus that all the world should be taxed. . . ."

The beautiful old story unfolded and spoke to us. After singing "Silent Night," 30 lonesome and hungry girls found the peace and blessing that only the Babe in Bethlehem can give: "Peace on earth and goodwill to men." Christmas had found its way into our war-torn hearts after all.

Christmas on the Homestead in 1894

Rosina Kiehlbauch

Two years ago, in Christmas in My Heart, *book 4, we began a true frontier Christmas trilogy, taken from the diaries of Rosina Kiehlbauch (a Dakota pioneer German from Russia who, with her family, experienced their first American Christmas in 1874). Catherine Sherry, a daughter, made them available to the American Historical Society of Germans from Russia, in Lincoln, Nebraska, who published them in their* Journal.

This year we complete the trilogy and note the almost mind-boggling changes that have taken place in but 20 years. I'd guess that those who have read the first two installments will, with me, be impressed by what the Kiehlbauchs have accomplished and become—and sigh at what they have lost.

Eighteen hundred and ninety-four. Another 10 years had passed, and the pioneer family was now living in a 12-room frame house in Tyndall, one of the prosperous little pioneer towns on the South Dakota prairie.

Johannes and Katharina Kiehlbauch had been blessed in their home, in their business and in the church. Their 11 children were well and happy, and Barbara, the eldest, was married and had presented them with two grandchildren. The younger children were still in the public school and stood high in their classes. The family's hardware and farm implement business was flourishing. The local white frame church with spire and bell, which they had helped build and in which Johannes was a deacon, attested to their firm belief in God.

The Christmas eve celebration in 1894 was the most elaborate ever held in the church. Young Johannes was on the committee to provide the tree. He decided that it should be the tallest tree that had ever stood in the church. He made a special trip to the Missouri River bluffs and cut the evergreen tree himself, but it required the ingenuity of several young men to help him bring the tree to town and set it up in the church without breaking any of its many branches.

The tree was truly a beautiful sight. It brought many "ahs" and "ohs" from the children on Christmas eve, when their starry eyes traveled from the lowest, heavily-decorated branches to the star-crowned tip that bent its head against the ceiling of the church.

There had been the exciting weeks of pre-Christmas practice, when boys and girls managed to walk to and from the church with their special friends. The usual jockeying for solo parts was comical to watch, and the young organist almost despaired at times, trying to reconcile the music as written by the composer and as sung by the volunteer choir. In addition, there was the drilling of the children on their recitations so that they would ascend the platform without stumbling, enunciate distinctly, put in a gesture or two and, above all, speak loudly enough so that the grandparents would be able to hear their darlings.

Finally, all the effort culminated in an unusual offering of songs, recitations, and dialogues for the Christmas eve program. Happy tears rolled down the cheeks of the Sunday school superintendent as he listened to the angelic voices of the little boys' class sing "*Stille Nacht.*" He was so pleased that on the second day of Christmas (the Germans from South Russia then still observed three days of Christmas) he gave each boy a quarter.

Another evergreen tree awaited the Kiehlbauch children when they returned home from church. It twinkled and glistened in the parlor, where it stood between the new piano and the large plate glass window framed by filmy Nottingham lace curtains. Next to it stood Katarina's pride and joy, a gorgeous Christmas cactus with a hundred flaming blossoms. At the foot of the tree were gifts and gifts and gifts.

The family assembled for prayers of thanksgiving before the presents were distributed. Beneath the wrappings they found mechanical toys, games, books, neckties, albums, decorated novelties of gilt, beads, and shells, embroidered sofa cushions, jewelry, dress goods, and an astrakhan fur coat for each of the big girls—Katya, Christie, and Leesa. Mother received a pink-flowered Haviland dinner set, and Father a rocking chair upholstered in dark green velvet, a gift from his Sunday school class. Plates of nuts and special Christmas cookies and candies, made by the older girls, stood in convenient places for nibbling.

After all the presents were unwrapped and admired, Leesa went to the piano, turned up the stool, arranged her skirts, and started to play. Johannes removed the elaborate red silk and lace lamp shade, adjusted the wick of the new piano lamp so that it gave the most light without smoking up the chimney. The shorter children pushed in front of the taller ones as the whole family gathered around the piano to sing again their favorite German Christmas songs.

After a while, the younger children, still conscious of their halos bestowed upon them because they had performed their parts in the Christmas program so well, quietly took their presents to the dining room to play. The dining room was the favorite place to play. There the hanging lamp shed plenty of light over the golden oak extension table that was arranged for games or study after supper. Monnie, one of the three younger boys who had been born since they had moved to town, piled his presents on a chair to leave his end of the oil-cloth-covered table free for running his noisy iron train. Willie had the middle of the table at his disposal for his fire engine. Rosina pulled up a kitchen table to the end of the dining room table to give Nettie, Johanna, and herself more room to spread out their books, watercolors, games, a toy stove with tin pans, and a pewter tea set. In the place of honor in the high chair she put a big sleeping doll with real hair, bisque head, arms, and feet. The doll was stylishly attired in a dress of white china silk, two starched petticoats with lace insertions, tucks, and many ruffles. The long drawers and the Lonsdale muslin chemise with a Valencionnes lace yoke completed the clothing made by the older girls. On her pink feet were beautiful kid slippers. Leo, the youngest of the brothers, set up his Noah's ark on the floor near the big, nickel-trimmed "Round Oak" heater that sent a cheerful glow through its elaborate mica-lined doors.

Monnie's long iron train was noisy, but Willie's red fire truck, with ladders and galloping horses, made even more noise. Once Willie gave the truck too energetic a start and the horses got out of hand and ran into the girls' array of presents. The pewter dishes, tin pans, horses, and truck clattered off the end of the table and scattered Leo's spindle-legged animals that were marching sedately into the ark. Such noises and crying evaporated all signs of childish halos, but fortunately there were no casualties beyond a dented teapot and a silenced singing top.

Mother and big sister Katya came and untangled the toys. Mother decided it was time for everyone to go to bed. She therefore took little Nettie and went to the bedrooms to light the kerosene lamps. Katya helped Johanna and Rosina unfasten the many buttons down the backs of their Christmas dresses and untie the ribbons from their long braids. Then Katya went to see whether "the boys," as the three younger brothers were called, had hung up their coats, Windsor ties, and beruffled blouses. For a bedtime story, Katya told them about the first Christmas at Clear Lake homestead.

"Not much of a Christmas, I'd say," commented Monnie. Katya made no reply. She had fond memories of which the three young lads had no knowledge. Meanwhile, Christie and Leesa carefully replaced the

young children's presents under the tree and straightened out the dining room, in readiness for the big Christmas dinner with the grandchildren and relatives that would follow the morning's church service.

After the older children had picked up their presents and gone to their rooms, the house was quiet. Johannes and Katharina sat for a while by the marble-topped center table in the sitting room, enjoying some of the Christmas goodies and talking about the many happy holidays they had celebrated in America. As Johannes was about to turn out the hanging lamp, he drew his hand over its rows of glass prisms and set them jingling. "Not much like the 'wild goose lamp' of the homestead days," he remarked.

"No, Johannes, no more like the 'wild goose lamp' of the prairie than tonight's Christmas was like our first Christmas in America in 1874. How far away that seems. We have come a long way, but we have lost something during the years—or is it only that we are older and times have changed and we have more to do with?"

"I also have been wondering," answered her husband thoughtfully. "Sometimes nothing seems like old times. Sometimes I imagine that even the wild geese that our son shoots each year for our family Christmas dinner don't taste as good as they used to. There is a difference somewhere, yet I wouldn't want to go back to the old days. One has the courage of youth only once."

"Yes, it seems different. But as you say, those days were good for their times, and the present days are good for the present time. Only children are the same—always looking forward, always anxious for the next day, always wanting something different. What do you think of this idea? I have been thinking it over for the last few days. Let's drive up to the farm after Christmas and get some willow branches and make a little willow Christmas tree to set next to the big tree when we light it again for the last time on New Year's eve. I could make little 'willowminna' dolls for each of the girls, and you could make willow tops, whistles, or hobby horses for the boys. It would show the younger children what we did that first Christmas in America, when that was all we had to work with."

"I do believe that you have never grown up, Katharina. What an excuse for playing with dolls!" teased her husband.

"I don't hear any objections to your making tops or whistles. So don't try to hide behind your wife's skirts."

"All right, my fingers are not stiff," answered Johannes. He drew his hand from his pocket. "I have here the best pocketknife that the trade offers, a Christmas gift from one of my hardware agents at the store. I'm willing to try my hand at being young again."

On New Year's eve, when the Christmas tree was lighted for the last time, the candles were adjusted very carefully, and the ever present bucket of water was placed within easy reach, in case it should be needed. The children were overjoyed to find that the New Year had brought a little willow Christmas tree, willowminna dolls, willow tops, whistles, and hobby horses, and a crock of silvery "papoose" pussy willow branches standing by the gorgeous, blossom-laden Christmas cactus. After the noise of the whistles and the prancing horses had ceased, the family settled down to relive some of the days of pioneering on the Clear Lake homestead.

On the stroke of 12:00, while the family was exchanging New Year's greetings, five shots rang out in quick succession in front of the house.

"Indians!" gleefully shouted young Johannes, still lost in pioneer days.

When his father opened the front door, the "Indians" turned out to be five townsmen with smoking guns. These recently arrived immigrants from South Russia had come to honor their fellow countrymen and the mayor of the town with the characteristic South Russian New Year's greetings—five shots fired in quick succession in front of the home of a person holding an important public office. Johannes, responding to the spirit of the occasion, invited his guests into the house and offered them the usual South Russian drink. Then, lest his well-meaning friends get into trouble with their new American freedoms, he explained to them some of the eccentricities of American ways, which, among other things, did not countenance shooting within city limits, even as a New Year's honor for the mayor. Then he thanked them for their well-meaning gesture, linking the old world tradition with the new.

As the guests departed, the leader again wished the mayor *"ein glückliches Neu Jahr"* and asked him to excuse the fireworks. He promised that the next year they would use the simple American greeting, "Happy New Year." Thus ended the holiday celebrations in 1894.

The Miraculous Staircase

Arthur Gordon

I first read this "legend" a number of years ago in The Guideposts Christmas Treasury, *then again in Mr. Gordon's wonderful collection of stories,* A Touch of Wonder. *I put the word "legend" in quotes because, unlike most legends, this particular one leaves one with so many unanswered questions.*

When I made my first visit to Santa Fe, at the top of my list of priorities was the Chapel of Our Lady of Light. I had to see that staircase! And suddenly, there it was. I could only stand there, blinking my eyes in disbelief.

Arthur Gordon (born in 1912), during his long and illustrious career, has edited such renowned journals as Good Housekeeping, Cosmopolitan, *and* Guideposts. *Along the way, besides penning over 200 of some of the finest short stories of our time, he also somehow found time to write books, such as* Reprisal, Norman Vincent Peale: Minister to Millions, *and* Red Carpet at the White House. *Today, he and his wife Pamela still live on the Georgia coast he has loved since he was a child. What a joy to welcome him to the family of* Christmas in My Heart *authors.*

On that cool December morning in 1878, sunlight lay like an amber rug across the dusty streets and adobe houses of Santa Fe. It glinted on the bright tile roof of the almost completed Chapel of Our Lady of Light and on the nearby windows of the convent school run by the Sisters of Loretto. Inside the convent, the Mother Superior looked up from her packing as a tap came on her door.

"It's *another* carpenter, Reverend Mother," said Sister Francis Louise, her round face apologetic. "I told him that you're leaving right away, that you haven't time to see him, but he says—"

"I know what he says," Mother Magdalene said, going on resolutely with her packing. "That he's heard about our problem with the new chapel. That he's the best carpenter in all of New Mexico. That he can build us a staircase to the choir loft despite the fact that the brilliant architect in Paris who drew the plans failed to leave any space for one. And despite the fact that five master carpenters have already tried and failed. You're quite right, Sister; I don't have time to listen to that story again."

"But he seems such a nice man," said Sister Francis Louise wistfully, "and he's out there with his burro, and—"

"I'm sure," said Mother Magdalene with a smile, "that he's a charming man, and that his burro is a charming donkey. But there's sickness down at the Santo Domingo pueblo, and it may be cholera. Sister Mary Helen and I are the only ones here who've had cholera. So we have to go. And you have to stay and run the school. And that's that!" Then she called, "Manuela!"

A young Indian girl of 12 or 13, black-haired and smiling, came in quietly on moccasined feet. She was a mute. She could hear and understand, but the Sisters had been unable to teach her to speak. The Mother Superior spoke to her gently. "Take my things down to the wagon, child. I'll be right there." And to Sister Francis Louise: "You'd better tell your carpenter friend to come back in two or three weeks. I'll see him then."

"Two or three weeks! Surely you'll be home for Christmas?"

"If it's the Lord's will, Sister. I hope so." In the street, beyond the waiting wagon, Mother Magdalene could see the carpenter, a bearded man, strongly built and taller than most Mexicans, with dark eyes and a smiling, wind-burned face. Beside him, laden with tools and scraps of lumber, a small gray burro stood patiently. Manuela was stroking its nose, glancing shyly at its owner.

"You'd better explain," said the Mother Superior, "that the child can hear him, but she can't speak."

Goodbyes were quick, the best kind when you leave a place you love. Southwest, then, along the dusty trail, the mountains purple with shadow, the Rio Grande a ribbon of green far off to the right. The pace was slow, but Mother Magdalene and Sister Mary Helen amused themselves by singing songs and telling Christmas stories as the sun marched up and down the sky. And their leathery driver listened and nodded.

Two days of this brought them to Santo Domingo Pueblo, where the sickness was not cholera after all, but measles, and almost as deadly in an Indian village. And

so they stayed, helping the harassed Father Sebastian, visiting the dark adobe hovels where feverish brown children tossed, and fierce Indian dogs showed their teeth.

At night they were bone weary, but sometimes Mother Magdalene found time to talk to Father Sebastian about her plans for the dedication of the new chapel. It was to be in April; the Archbishop himself would be there. And it might have been dedicated sooner, were it not for this incredible business of a choir loft with no means of access—unless it were a ladder.

"I told the Bishop," said Mother Magdalene, "that it would be a mistake to have the plans drawn in Paris. If something went wrong, what could we do? But he wanted our chapel in Santa Fe patterned after the Sainte Chapelle in Paris, and who am I to argue with Bishop Lamy? So the talented Monsieur Mouly designs a beautiful choir loft high up under the rose window, and no way to get up to it."

"Perhaps," sighed Father Sebastian, "he had in mind a heavenly choir. The kind with wings."

"It's not funny," said Mother Magdalene a bit sharply. "I've prayed and prayed, but apparently there's no solution at all. There just isn't room on the chapel floor for the supports such a staircase needs."

The days passed, and with each passing day Christmas drew closer. Twice, horsemen on their way from Santa Fe to Albuquerque brought letters from Sister Francis Louise. All was well at the convent, but Mother Magdalene frowned over certain paragraphs. "The children are getting ready for Christmas," Sister Francis Louise wrote in her first letter. "Our little Manuela and the carpenter have become great friends. It's amazing

how much he seems to know about us all. . . ."

And what, thought Mother Magdalene, *is the carpenter still doing there?*

The second letter also mentioned the carpenter. "Early every morning he comes with another load of lumber, and every night he goes away. When we ask him by what authority he does these things, he smiles and says nothing. We have tried to pay him for his work, but he will accept no pay. . . ."

Work? What work? Mother Magdalene wrinkled up her nose in exasperation. Had that softhearted Sister Francis Louise given the man permission to putter around in the new chapel? With a firm and disapproving hand the Mother Superior wrote a note ordering an end to all such unauthorized activities. She gave it to an Indian pottery maker on his way to Santa Fe.

But that night the first snow fell, so thick and heavy that the Indian turned back. Next day at noon the sun shone again on a world glittering with diamonds. But Mother Magdalene knew that another snowfall might make it impossible for her to be home for Christmas. By now the sickness at Santo Domingo was subsiding. And so that afternoon they began the long ride back.

The snow did come again, making their slow progress even slower. It was late on Christmas Eve, close to midnight, when the tired horses plodded up to the convent door. But lamps still burned. Manuela flew down the steps, Sister Francis Louise close behind her. And chilled and weary though she was, Mother Magdalene sensed instantly an excitement, an electricity in the air that she could not understand. Nor did she understand it when they led her, still in her heavy wraps, down the corridor, into the new,

51

as yet unused chapel where a few candles burned.

"Look, Reverend Mother," breathed Sister Francis Louise. "Look!"

Like a curl of smoke the staircase rose before them, as insubstantial as a dream. Its base was on the chapel floor; its top rested against the choir loft. Nothing else supported it; it seemed to float on air. There were no banisters. Two complete spirals it made, the polished wood gleaming softly in the candlelight.

"Thirty-three steps," whispered Sister Francis Louise. "One for each year in the life of Our Lord."

Mother Magdalene moved forward like a woman in a trance. She put her foot on the first step, then the second, then the third. There was not a tremor. She looked down, bewildered, at Manuela's ecstatic, upturned face. "But it's impossible! There wasn't time!"

"He finished yesterday," the Sister said. "He didn't come today. No one has seen him anywhere in Santa Fe. He's gone."

"But *who* was he? Don't you even know his name?"

The Sister shook her head, but now Manuela pushed forward, nodding emphatically. Her mouth opened; she took a deep, shuddering breath; she made a sound that was like a gasp in the stillness. The nuns stared at her, transfixed. She tried again. This time it was a syllable, followed by another. "José." She clutched the Mother Superior's arm and repeated the first word she had ever spoken. "José!"

Sister Francis Louise crossed herself. Mother Magdalene felt her heart contract. José, the Spanish word for Joseph. Joseph the Carpenter. Joseph the Master Woodworker of—

"José!" Manuela's dark eyes were full of tears. "José!"

Silence, then, in the shadowy chapel. No one moved. Far away across the snow-silvered town Mother Magdalene heard a bell tolling midnight. She came down the stairs and took Manuela's hand. She felt uplifted by a great surge of wonder and gratitude and compassion and love. And she knew what it was. It was the spirit of Christmas. And it was upon them all.

Author's Note: The wonderful thing about legends is the way they grow. Through the years they can be told and retold and embroidered a bit more each time. This, indeed, is such a retelling. But all good legends contain a grain of truth, and in this case the irrefutable fact at the heart of the legend is the inexplicable staircase itself.

You may see it for yourself in Santa Fe today. It stands just as it stood when the chapel was dedicated almost 90 years ago, except for the banister, which was added later. Tourists stare and marvel. Architects shake their heads and murmur, "Impossible." No one knows the identity of the designer-builder. All the Sisters know is that the problem existed, a stranger came, solved it, and left. The 33 steps make two complete turns without central support. There are no nails in the staircase; only wooden pegs. The curved stringers are put together with exquisite precision; the wood is spliced in seven places on the inside, and nine on the outside. The wood is said to be a hard fir variety, nonexistent in New Mexico. School records show that no payment for the staircase was ever made.

Who is real and who is imaginary in this version of the story? Mother Mary Magdalene was indeed the first Mother

Superior. She came to Santa Fe by riverboat and covered wagon in 1852. Bishop J. B. Lamy was indeed her Bishop (best known to us as the real life clergyman on which Willa Cather based her literary classic, Death Comes to the Archbishop). And Monsieur Projectus Mouly of Paris was indeed the absentminded architect.

Sister Francis Louise? Well, there must have been someone like her. And Manuela, the Indian girl, came out of nowhere to help with the embroidery.

The carpenter himself? Ah, who can say?

The Stuffed Kitten

Mae Hurley Ashworth

I don't know why it is, but oftentimes some of the most memorable stories turn out to be the shortest ones. I know, for I've tried to write short ones, but have never been able to pull it off. I'm convinced that the best ones are divine gifts; they are just given to you.

One of those rare few is this one; and it first came to me many years ago. Like "Christmas in Tin Can Valley," it seemed to me early on that it was too short and too simple to warrant inclusion. But it has been a burr under my saddle every year—in its quiet, gentle but determined way, nosing itself into my decision chamber. Since I have been a teacher for more than a third of a century and know whereof Ashworth speaks, I cringe every time I read it. It really says it all.

I have never been able to find out anything about the author.

Each year at Christmas time I set out upon the mantel a little old shabby, stuffed toy kitten. It's good for laughs among my friends. They don't know, you see, that the kitten is a kind of memorial to a child who taught me the true meaning and spirit of living.

The stuffed kitten came into my life when I was quite young and teaching third grade. It was the day before the Christmas holidays, and at the last recess I was unwrapping the gifts the children had brought me. The day was cold and rainy; so the boys and girls had remained indoors, and they crowded around my desk to watch.

I opened the packages with appropriate exclamations of gratitude over lacy handkerchiefs, pink powder puffs, candy boxes, and other familiar Christmas tributes to teacher.

Finally, the last gift had been admired and the children began drifting away. I started to work on plans for an after-holidays project. When I looked up again, only one child remained at the table looking at the gifts. She did not touch anything. Her arms were stiff at her sides, but her head bent forward a little so that the thick, jagged locks of her dust-colored hair hung over her eyes.

Poor Agnes, I thought. She looked like a small, dazzled sheepdog.

I had always felt a little guilty about Agnes because, no matter how hard I tried, I couldn't help being annoyed by her. She was neither pretty nor winsome, and her stupidity in class was exhausting. Most of all, her unrestrained affection offended me. She had a habit of twining her soiled little fingers around my hand, or patting my arm, or fingering my dress. Of course, I never actually pushed her away. Dutifully, I endured her love.

"Well, Agnes?" I said now.

Abruptly she walked back to her seat, but a moment later I found her beside me again—clutching a toy stuffed kitten. The kitten's skin was dismal yellow

rayon, and its eyes were bright red beads. Agnes thrust it toward me in an agony of emotion. "It's for you," she whispered. "I couldn't buy you anything."

Her face was alive as I had never seen it before. Her eyes, usually dull, were shining. Under the sallowness of her skin spread a faint tinge of pink.

I felt dismayed. Not only did the kitten hold no charms for me, but I sensed that it was Agnes' own new and treasured possession, probably about the only Christmas she'd have.

So I said, "Oh, no, Agnes, you keep it for yourself!"

The shine fled from her eyes and her shoulders drooped. "You—don't you like this kitten?"

I put on my heartiest manner. "Of course, I like it, Agnes. If you are sure you want me to have it, why thank you!"

She set the kitten on its ill-made, wobbly legs, atop my desk. And the look on her face—I'll never forget it—was one of abject gratitude.

That afternoon, when the children were preparing to go home, Agnes detached herself from the line at the lockers and came over to my desk. She pushed her moist little hand into mine and whispered, "I'm glad you like the kitten. You *do* like it, don't you?"

I could sense her reaching out for warmth and approval, and I tried to rise to the occasion. "It's quite the nicest desk ornament I've ever had. Now run along, Agnes." I remembered to add, "And have a Merry Christmas."

I watched the children as they marched out and scattered. Agnes started alone down the walk, the rain pelting her bare head.

She was never to return to school. On her way home, a reckless driver ended the small life that had gone almost unnoticed in our community.

On Christmas day I went to my deserted schoolroom to face the stuffed kitten—and to have it out with my own sick conscience. Confession is healing, and I felt better after I had poured out my remorse to Agnes' mute gift. The giver was gone, beyond reach of the love and encouragement she had so desperately needed and that I could have given her.

Or could I have—without Agnes' gift, and without her tragedy? Sometimes the capacity for responding to another's need comes only when the soul is *forced* to expand.

From now on, I promised the stuffed kitten, I would make children my life, not just my living. Besides teaching them the facts found in books, I would look into their hearts with love and with understanding. I'd give them myself, as well as my knowledge.

And heaven help me if I should ever again recoil from a grubby, seeking hand!

Matthew, Mark, Luke, and John

Pearl S. Buck

War. Besides all the blood, anguish, and devastation it leaves in its wake, it also leaves those. Twelve-year-old Matthew was one of those, struggling to stay alive in the bitterly cold winter, hiding under a bridge. And then there was Mark; now there were two to feed. And then, with Luke, three. And last, with John, four! What was he to do?

Of all the stories to come out of the Korean War, this is one of the most poignant, most moving. Pulitzer and Nobel Prize winner Pearl Buck bridged, perhaps better than any other American author, that vast cultural chasm separating East from West. With each year that has passed we have received more requests to include this moving Pearl Buck story in our next collection.

Its time has come.

He woke early. The rumble of trucks and cars, the trotting of donkeys' feet, the slow thud of a horse's hooves, sounded on the bridge above his head. It was the beginning of another day.

"My name is Matthew," he said.

He spoke the words aloud and slowly, so that he would not forget them. They were the only English words he knew because he was in Korea. Here he had been born, his father an American soldier, and here he had lived for all the 11 years of his life. He lived alone now under a bridge in the city of Pusan. When he had lost his Korean mother, nearly a year ago, he had taken shelter under the old stone bridge in a pounding rainstorm.

He could not understand how he had lost his mother. Or had she lost him? They were very poor, he remembered. They lived in a small earthen house in a village with her parents. He knew they were her parents for she called them "Father" and "Mother," but what he could not understand was that he was never allowed to call them "Grandfather" and "Grandmother," even though his cousins did so. Only his mother could be called by name.

"Why can I not call the others by name?" he had asked his mother.

"Because your father was an American," she had replied. "Therefore, you belong to him, not to us. Children in Korea belong to the father. His name was Matthew, and I gave you his name."

"What is American?" he had asked his mother. "I do not know what it is."

"It means someone from America," his mother had replied. "Someone different from us. You look like him. Your eyes are too light, your hair is too red. Here in Korea we have black eyes and hair."

"Do you mind?" he had asked.

He had watched her face to see if she minded. Sometimes other children teased him and called him "Foreigner," or even "Round-eyes." She had only pursed her lips. Then she had smiled. "How would you like to go to the city tomorrow?" she had asked. "I will buy you a new jacket."

He forgot his first question in another. "But do you have enough money for that, Mother?" he asked.

She put her hand into her inner pocket and said, "I have saved enough from my sewing."

It was the next day that he remembered to ask the next question. In the excitement of buying the new jacket, he had thought of nothing else. His old jacket had been too small for a long time. When he put on the new one in the shop it was too big, and he felt lost in its looseness.

"It must last you for a very long time," his mother had said. "I may never be able to buy you another." Tears came into her eyes, and she wiped them away with the edge of her wide sleeve.

He had been frightened. "I am not going to die, am I?" he had asked.

She had tried to laugh, but the tears kept coming. She looked at him in his new jacket. "I wish your father could see you," she said.

It was then he thought of the next question. "Where is my father?"

She had shaken her head. "He went away to America."

The shopkeeper had been listening. Now he spoke. "Ah, he is one of those!"

"Yes," his mother replied.

She counted out the money for the jacket and they left the shop. The street was crowded, and he walked behind her, as usual. For some reason she never let him walk beside her. Since he had learned to walk this was her rule and he obeyed. Suddenly she stopped and turned to him.

"Stay here," she told him. "I paid the shopkeeper three pennies too much. I must go back and get those pennies. Here—hold my purse."

She thrust the small bag of coins into his hand and hurried away. He waited a long time, and when he grew tired he sat down on the edge of the curb, tucking up his jacket to keep it from the dust. The sun had been shining straight down into the street when she left him, and now it had slipped behind the houses. The shadows were chill and he was hungry. He searched the face of each passerby, but his mother never appeared.

At last he rose to his feet. It occurred to him that he should go back to the shop and see if his mother were there. He thought he knew the way, but when he tried to remember where the turns were, he was soon lost. He never found the shop, although he had often tried to do so, and never again had he seen his mother's face, though he kept looking.

That first night he had crept under the bridge and cried himself to sleep. Now, of course, he knew better than to cry. He had made himself a sort of home there, and he came back to it every night. Still, when he woke in the morning, as he did now, he always had a moment or two of feeling lost again. He was quite alone, and sometimes he wished that he had a friend, a boy like himself. There were such boys, he knew, for more than once someone would stare at him and mutter, "Another one of those!"

The cave under the bridge was big enough for another boy, maybe even two or three. It was convenient to have water so near, but in winter the river froze. He had learned how to make a fire in the back of the cave and to melt ice in a tin can he had found in a garbage pail outside the American camp. He knew now what an American was, for sometimes an American soldier gave him a coin for polishing his shoes, or just for begging, after the money his mother had given him was gone. He tried not to think about his mother. Had she wanted to find him as he wanted to find her? For days, for months, he had searched the passing faces. He had given up at last, and he had only this pain in his heart if he let himself think of her.

He got up now and lit a little fire to heat his food. This morning he had rice left over from yesterday and some kimchee he had bought. It was a windy autumn morning and the smoke blew out from under the bridge. He heard footsteps, and in a moment someone appeared at the nearest arch of the bridge. It was a policeman.

"You, redhead," the policeman called. "What have I told you about making a big fire? Do you want me to lose my job? It is forbidden to build fires under bridges."

"It is a big wind, not a big fire," Matthew said.

But he covered the fire with some ash. The policeman was kind and let him live under the bridge. Sometimes he even brought Matthew a small bag of rice or a round bun of bread stuffed with meat. Today he tossed the boy a coin.

"Buy yourself some socks," he said. "Winter is coming."

Winter! Matthew dreaded the winter. In spite of the fire, he could never get warm. He thought of this as he ate his rice and kimchee now. Perhaps if he could earn a little more money he could go to the pawnshop and buy an old quilt to spread on top of his straw bed. It had not been easy to get even the straw. People bought it to burn in their kitchens, and he snatched handfuls at a time from the bundles farmers brought into the city to sell. Sometimes they caught him and cuffed his ears.

"Foreign brat!" they bawled at him.

Why was he foreign? He thought about this as he washed after breakfast. The river water was already cold, and his skin felt cold as the wind dried it.

It was a bright day, he discovered, when he came out from under the bridge. The sun never reached his cave, but now the day was heartening. Already the sun was warm. The street was busy with morning life. Shops were open, people were coming and going. It was the season for ripe persimmons, and when he passed a pile beside someone's doorway he longed to pick up a few, except that it might be stealing. But was it stealing when they were everywhere? Sometimes people were kind and would even give him a persimmon. More often they set the dogs on him.

And as he walked he considered what he could do to earn some money to buy a quilt. His luck was always at the U.S. Army camp. There, though he was never allowed inside the guarded gate, the American men coming and going sometimes gave him money—or a foreign magazine or some cigarettes, either of which he could sell. It was still early when he got to the camp and he prepared himself to wait there in patience.

He was no sooner there, however, than a strange

thing happened. A woman came running out of the gate, sobbing as she ran. She was young and a Korean, wearing a full dark red skirt and a white Korean silk bodice. He saw this as she stumbled and sank down on the ground, her long black hair in its braid falling over her shoulder into the dust.

"Aie, aie," she sobbed.

"Why are you crying?" he called out.

She lifted her head and stared at him, her eyes wide and wet with tears. "Another one of them!" she sobbed, and getting to her feet she ran on until she was lost in the crowd.

This was puzzling enough, but in a few moments an American in uniform came out of the gate leading a small boy by the hand. He was not a very small boy, perhaps 6 or 7 years old, and he was neatly dressed in short dark trousers and a red sweater. He did not look Korean, but neither did he look American as the man did.

The American looked left and right and down the street. "Was that your mother?" he asked the boy in Korean. "Where did she go?"

It was not very good Korean, but Matthew could understand it. The boy shook his head. Matthew answered for him, of course, in Korean, since he spoke no English except for his name. He pointed to the distance. "She ran that way."

The man looked at him. "What's your name, boy?"

"My name is Matthew."

The man said, unbelievingly, "Matthew? For a Korean boy?"

"I am also American," Matthew said.

The man gave a great sigh. "Then here is your brother. His name had better be Mark. 'Matthew, Mark, Luke, and John, the beds be blessed that you lie on—'" His face twisted as though in sudden pain. He felt in his pocket, brought out a fistful of money, and stuffed it into Mark's pocket. Then he turned and marched back inside the gate.

The two boys stood looking at each other. Matthew saw a sturdy boy with a round face, rosy cheeks, bright brown eyes, and short, golden brown hair. He was not at all thin, and he looked very clean, as though he had just come from a bath, and his clothes were new, even his shoes.

"Is your name Mark?" Matthew asked.

The boy looked at him as though he did not understand.

"Mark?" Matthew repeated.

The boy smiled. He had a nice cheerful smile, and his name must be Mark, Matthew decided, since he did not deny it.

"Where do you live?" Matthew asked.

Mark looked at him, not answering. He was still smiling, but now uncertainly. Suddenly Matthew understood. Mark could not speak Korean! And he, Matthew, could not speak English. What could they do? For a moment he thought he would go on his way. As soon as he began to walk down the street, however, Mark ran after him and clung to his hand. He looked at Matthew and tears came into his eyes. He poured out English words, trying not to cry.

"I don't know what you're saying," Matthew replied. "But you had better come with me."

He took Mark's hand and led him toward the

bridge. Suddenly he thought of the money Mark had in his pocket. Now that there were two of them, they really would have to buy a quilt, a big one that would cover two boys instead of one. He stopped at a pawnshop and, hand in hand, they went in.

An old man in a patched white robe stood behind the counter. "What do you want?" he asked.

"A quilt, big enough for two," Matthew replied. "And it must be thick and warm."

"You are very small to be buying your own quilt," the old man said.

"We are orphans," Matthew said to him.

The old man picked up a pair of iron-rimmed spectacles from the counter, put them on, and stared at the boys.

"Ah, you are two of those," he said then.

"Yes," Matthew replied.

"Are you brothers?" the old man asked.

Matthew hesitated. Then he answered out of his heart. "Yes, at least we are going to be. I just found him today."

The old man shook his head. "I don't understand that, but never mind. The important question is, have you money?"

Matthew turned to Mark. "Give me the money," he said, and pointed to Mark's pocket. Mark understood. He took out the handful of bills and gave them to Matthew.

"How much is a quilt?" Matthew asked.

The old man's eyes were greedy at the sight of so much money, but he was still good enough to remember that these were two lonely children. "First choose the quilt," he said. "Then let us talk of the price."

Matthew felt the quilts the old man brought out and selected the thickest. It was covered with gray cotton cloth and patched in only a few places.

"We will take this," he said. "How much is it?"

The old man struggled with himself, and then gave up the idea of asking too much money. "It is a good quilt," he said. "I could sell it for a great deal of money now that winter is near. But since you are orphans, I will give it to you for one-third the price."

"Thank you," Matthew said.

He paid for it, took the quilt in his arms, and Mark held the edge of his coat instead of his hand.

Together they went to the bridge. Inside the cave the light was dim, but everything Matthew had was there: his wooden box with a few clothes (he had begged the box from a shopkeeper), some pictures he had torn out of an old magazine, his chopsticks and the round tin cans he used for food bowls, and the old tin teakettle he had found on a trash heap. He spread the quilt over his heap of straw, and then sat admiring the cave. It really looked nice, he thought, now that they had the quilt. And there was still some money left. He counted it and, taking out only a little for food, he put the rest in his secret hole behind a loose stone.

All this time, while he had been busy, Mark was sitting on a ledge watching him and saying nothing, because he could not speak Korean. Now Matthew sat on the ledge too, to think what to do. How could he live with someone with whom he could not talk? He wished so much to ask Mark who he really was, why he was able to have such good clothes, who the woman was who ran away sobbing, why he could not speak Korean, how he happened to be in a camp. Not one question could he ask. He would simply have to teach Mark how to speak in Korean. Well, then he had better begin. His eyes fell on Mark's neat new shoes. He pointed to them.

"Shoes," he said in Korean.

"Shoes," Mark repeated in Korean.

Thus was begun their new life together. Slowly, slowly, a day at a time, word after word, Mark learned to speak Korean. And word after word, too, Matthew learned English. In a very few weeks he wondered how he had ever lived without Mark. *I must have been very lonely without knowing it,* he thought.

Indeed he had been very lonely, for Korean boys teased him on the streets, and he had learned to avoid them, preferring loneliness to their shouts and laughter because, they said, he looked so strange. Now he had Mark, and they were never separated. By day they begged or worked, when they could find work, such as sweeping the street in front of a shop. Begging was easier now that there were two of them, especially begging from Americans, who gave them money and sometimes bread and other foods. Sometimes, too, they did not like the foods, but they ate them anyway, for food is food.

It was not long before Mark learned to speak Korean easily, and though English was harder, Matthew learned, and after a few months the two boys had no trouble in talk.

By now, too, it was winter. Snow fell and the wind blew in from the cold gray sea or down from the mountains behind the city. They slept warmly enough together under the quilt, but in the day they had to get food somehow. There were times when Mark cried because he was so cold. His hands were swollen with frost-

bite, and Matthew kept careful watch of his cheeks and nose. Matthew decided that he must build some sort of shelter. But where could he find materials without stealing them? He was afraid to steal, for his mother had taught him this was something he must not do.

At last he decided to talk with the policeman. Now and again the policeman called under the bridge to see how the boys fared. Sometimes he said they should go to an orphanage, but Matthew begged him to leave them where they were.

"But this second one is very small," the policeman argued. "See him shivering with cold!"

"I take care of him," Matthew said proudly. "We need a few boards and something to keep the wind from the cracks between. Then we will be warm."

The policeman went away grumbling, but after the next snowstorm he came back. "They are taking down some old huts to put up a new building," he told Matthew. "It is near here, and you may carry away some boards. It is not my affair if a few boards are taken."

So Matthew and Mark carried boards, and the policeman gave them a handful of nails and Matthew used a round stone for a hammer. He put up a wall of boards and he found old paper on the streets and filled the cracks, and the wind no longer circled the cave under the bridge. In the winter nights the two boys talked together as they lay under the quilt, and Matthew learned Mark's story.

"My mother and I lived in Seoul," he told Matthew, "and my father in America sent us money. He sent enough for food and clothes, and we lived in a nice room. We spoke only English, and my mother did not let me play with other children. We had only each other. Then suddenly my father stopped sending money. My mother wrote him, and he wrote back to tell her he was married now to an American wife. Another American man came to see my mother, but my mother would not talk to him. At first she would not talk, but when we had no more money, she did talk to him. The man put me out of the room so he could talk to my mother at night. I sat on the street waiting for them to stop talking. Sometimes I went to sleep while I waited. She cried, but we had no money except from this man. One day he went away, too. She heard that he had been sent to the camp in Pusan, and so we came here. All our money was gone when we reached the camp. But the man was not at the camp. Some other man, an officer, was rough to my mother. He told her to get out. So she ran to the gate because she was afraid and I could not run so fast. I fell down and another man helped me and took me to the gate. But she was gone. He was the one who named me Mark. Who was Mark?"

"I don't know any Mark except you," Matthew said. "And who is Luke and who is John?"

"I don't know them," Mark said.

Mark was sleepy now and he fell asleep, curled against Matthew, to keep warm. But Matthew lay awake, thinking about himself and about Mark. Other people were all born into families, it seemed, and only they were born alone, without a family to care for them. How did it happen that they were born? Why was it that their fathers came from far away, strange men who were different from Korean men? And why could their Korean mothers not keep them? And why, oh why, did

63

other boys laugh at him and Mark and tease them as though they were homeless dogs? He asked himself such questions, but he could not answer one of them, and so at long last he fell asleep.

Somehow the winter passed. Snow ceased to fall, the wind blew less bitter, and along the roads outside the city small, green weeds struggled toward the light. Matthew and Mark were hungry for green vegetables, and they joined other poor people to dig the weeds to cook and eat with rice or millet. The birds, silent all through the winter, came back with the spring, and sang their songs again. The mountains, shedding their winter snows, lifted their gray heads against the blue sky.

All might have been almost happy for Matthew and Mark except that one evening, when they came back to the city, their basket heaped with dandelion, shepherd's purse, and young clover, their friend, the policeman, was waiting for them at the bridge. He was not alone. With one hand he grasped the torn collar of the jacket of a boy. One might have thought he was frightened, this boy, except for his eyes. They were large, round, and blue.

"Here is another one of those, like you," the policeman said. "I have just caught him. He was stealing the money out of a beggar's bowl—that old blind beggar who sits always at the temple gate yonder."

"I don't know this boy," Matthew said.

"I never saw him before," Mark said.

The boy looked from one face to the other, his bright eyes darting here and there. He had a round, naughty face; his brown hair was dusty, and he was very dirty. But he did not look hungry or thin.

"I ought to put him in jail," the policeman said.

"Don't put him in jail, please," Matthew said. "I can see that he is one of us. He can live in our cave. There is room for one more."

The policeman made his face stern. "What will you do if he steals again? He is a thief, and a clever one. See how fat he is? You are both thin, but he, he is a bad one."

"We will give him some of our food," Matthew said. "Look at our basket—it is spring now, and we can dig greens. And we can all work. He will work, too. People want to make gardens and plant seeds. We can do that."

The policeman put on an angry face. "What will you do if he won't work?"

"Let us try," Matthew said. He took the boy's hand. "Will you try?" he asked.

The boy nodded.

"Well, for a while," the policeman agreed. "Here, take this." He gave Matthew a piece of money and went away.

The three boys looked at each other.

"What is your name?" Matthew asked the new boy.

"I have no name," the boy said.

"What do people call you?" Matthew asked.

"They don't call me. I have no people," the boy said.

"No mother?" Mark asked.

"I've forgotten," the boy said.

"Where do you live?" Mark asked.

"Nowhere," the boy said.

"But at night?" Matthew urged.

"In a doorway; sometimes in the railroad station, but they chase me out."

"Come into the cave," Matthew said.

They crept under the bridge and into the cave.

"This is nice," the boy said, looking around.

During the winter Matthew and Mark had indeed tried to make the cave more comfortable. They had found some old boxes for seats, and they had found a board for a table.

"It is better than nothing," Matthew said proudly, "and you can sleep under our quilt with us. It is big enough for three. And your name will be Luke."

"What is Luke?" the boy asked.

"It is a name," Matthew said, "an American name. I can see your father was an American, like ours. We are those. That is what people call us here—*those*."

Now began a new life in the cave because of Luke. Before he came, Matthew and Mark had lived together without quarreling, Mark always obedient because Matthew was taller and older. But Luke obeyed no one. He had lived by stealing instead of working, and he did not like to work. When Matthew found a job for the three of them in a fruit shop, putting the fruit away at night and sweeping the floor, Luke did not do his share. And on the second day Matthew saw him put out his hand quickly and steal an orange and hide it in his pocket.

"Luke!" he shouted.

Luke was startled, and people turned their heads at the shout. Matthew did not know what to do. If he made Luke put the orange back everyone would know Luke was a thief and the policeman would put him in jail. He said nothing until they got back to the cave, and then he talked to Luke.

"You must not steal," he told Luke. "I am ashamed that you steal. If you steal you will be put in jail. Where is the orange? I will take it back."

"I ate it," Luke said. "And why shouldn't I steal? That old man will never miss an orange. I like oranges."

They were sitting around their box table eating their supper. Luke ate more than the others, and he kept on eating very fast.

"Besides," he said, his mouth full of rice and cabbage, "Mark ate part of the orange."

Matthew turned to Mark. "Did you?"

"Yes," Mark said in a small voice. "Luke told me to eat some."

"Didn't you know it was wrong?"

Matthew's voice was so stern that tears came into Mark's eyes and rolled down his cheeks. "You didn't tell me before," he said in a whisper.

"But I thought you knew, by yourself," Matthew said. "Did we ever steal anything before Luke came?"

Mark could not speak. He shook his head.

That night Matthew could not sleep. He turned and tossed because he did not know what to do. Luke would teach Mark how to steal. Mark was gentle and younger than Luke. Matthew decided to go and see the friendly policeman.

It was near midnight when he crept out from under the quilt. He left the two boys sleeping, and he came from under the bridge and went down the street and around the corner to where the policeman was on duty.

"There you are," the policeman said when he saw Matthew in the light of the street lamps. "Why are you out so late?"

"I am looking for you," Matthew said, and he told him his trouble.

The policeman leaned against the wall and listened. "I was afraid of this," he said. "Luke has been alone in the world since he was little, and he is used to stealing to live."

"Where is his mother?" Matthew asked.

"His mother is a thief, too, and she is in jail. They used to steal together."

"Doesn't he have a grandfather or an uncle or someone?" Matthew asked.

"They don't want him," the policeman said. "He is one of those. You had better let me put him in jail."

"No," Matthew said.

"Why won't you go into an orphanage?" the policeman asked. "They will feed you and clothe you."

"It is more like a family as we are," Matthew said.

"Then you are responsible for Luke," the policeman said. "As though you were his father."

"I will be responsible for him as though I were his father," Matthew said, and he walked alone through the quiet moonlit streets back to the cave again. What would he do if Luke would not change?

For a few days Luke was good. He even tried to help in sweeping out the fruit shop. Matthew began to hope that Luke would not steal anything again. Then it happened. It was night. They were getting ready for bed. Luke pulled off his jacket, and under it Matthew saw a new cotton shirt. His own had long since worn out.

"Where did you get that shirt?" he asked.

"A man gave it to me," Luke said.

Matthew looked straight into Luke's eyes. "Luke, is that true?"

"I have one, too," Mark said. He pulled open his jacket. "Luke gave it to me."

"Where did you get the shirts, Luke?" Matthew asked.

Luke tried to laugh. "Don't act so big, Matthew," he said. "You are not really our father."

"Take that shirt off," Matthew said. "Take yours off, Mark. Now, Luke, tell me where you got those shirts."

For a moment Luke stared back at Matthew, trying to be bold, and then his eyes fell. He peeled off the shirt slowly.

"I did it for Mark," he muttered.

"You did it for yourself," Matthew said. "And you hurt Mark because you are teaching him to steal. I cannot allow you to do this. I am responsible for you."

"What means responsible?" Mark asked.

"It means that if Luke steals, the policemen will blame me," Matthew said.

Luke looked surprised. "But you don't steal."

"No," Matthew said. "Of course, I don't steal. I would be ashamed to steal."

Luke looked puzzled.

"Do you understand?" Matthew asked.

"No," Luke said.

Matthew sighed. "We had better go to sleep," he said. "Tomorrow I will get up early. I will take back the shirts."

The next day he did take back the shirts. He explained everything to the shopkeeper.

"Keep the shirts," the shopkeeper said. "I cannot sell them now because they have been worn. But you are an honest boy."

"I will pay for them as soon as I can save the money," Matthew said.

Time passed. The summer came and went. It was autumn again. The leaves fell, persimmons ripened and lay in golden piles under the trees, in courtyards, and streets. Luke had been almost good all summer, but the persimmons were a temptation. There were so many of them everywhere; they were sweet with juice and Luke liked them too much. Again and again he ran off and came back with yellow stains about his mouth.

Matthew was angry and sad at the same time. Worst of all, Mark came back one day with yellow stains.

"Mark, did you steal?" Matthew demanded.

"Luke gave me some persimmons," Mark said. His round face was so innocent that Matthew said no more. Persimmons were plentiful, and perhaps he should not be too angry. But he was still not happy, and he went back to the policeman.

"Is taking persimmons stealing?" he asked.

"It's very near," the policeman said. "Is it that boy again? Once a thief, always a thief!"

Matthew went away quickly then. Persimmon time would soon be over. Then he must watch Luke very carefully as winter came on. Life was always harder in winter. Snow fell, winds blew, and work was scarce.

On top of everything else, they found John. It was a rainy afternoon, and they were out looking for food. Sometimes rich people threw quite good food away in garbage pails. Then dogs and poor people would snatch it for themselves.

"Let's go to that Choi family house," Luke said. "Sometimes they throw away bones with meat still left on them."

To the Choi house they went. No one was at the back gate when they arrived. No one? There was a very small boy there, hiding behind a crooked pine tree. He was eating a rotten pear. As soon as Matthew saw him, he recognized him. He was one of those. He had brown skin, but his eyes were gray and his hair was not black.

"Who are you?" Matthew asked.

The little boy was frightened. He could not have been more than 5 years old. He dropped the pear.

"I don't know," he said.

"What is your name?" Mark asked.

"I have no name," the boy said.

"Where do you live?" Luke asked.

"Nowhere," the child replied.

"And your mother, where is she?" Matthew asked.

"Mother? What is that?" the little boy asked in reply.

"Oh, let him come with us," Mark cried.

Matthew hesitated. Yet another? But in the end, of course, the little boy did go back with them to the cave. And since they found the skeleton of a chicken and some pork ribs with meat left on them, they had food.

"What shall we call our new brother?" Mark asked.

"We will call him John," Matthew said.

But in his heart he felt frightened. Three children, younger than he, all looking to him for food and clothes and shelter. . . . It was difficult to be a father. He began to understand why sometimes fathers went away and left their children. Well, he would never go away nor leave these three who trusted him and had no one else.

The next day was especially cold. The air was still and great flakes of snow began to fall. The four boys had no money for food, and there was no work to be had.

"Let's go by the American camp," Mark suggested.

"Remember the man at the gate gave us some money?"

"We are not beggars," Matthew said.

"No, we are only hungry," Mark replied.

There was nothing else to do, and so they went to the gate of the American camp. To their surprise, many children were going in.

"Let's go with them," Mark said eagerly.

Matthew hesitated. These children were all warmly dressed, and they looked well-fed.

"We don't belong with them," he said.

Just then the same American who had given them money came to the gate. "Hurry up, kids," he said. "Santa Claus is waiting. Lots of goodies for everybody!"

He pushed the four boys along with the others to a big room. It was warm and the air was fragrant with pine branches on the walls. In the middle of the room was a tall pine tree covered with small bright lights and ornaments. Beside the tree was an old man in a red suit. He had a long white beard.

"Santa Claus, Santa Claus," the American kept saying.

He pushed the children toward the old man with the long white beard, and as each passed, the old man gave the child a package.

To Matthew, Mark, Luke, and John he gave packages, too. In each was a pair of warm socks, a pair of warm gloves, some candy, and an apple. The boys could not believe what they saw. For besides these gifts there was food—cakes and nuts, rice and meat and hard-boiled eggs. And each could eat as much as he wished. Even Matthew forgot himself and ate until he could eat no more. The room was so warm that he was too hot and sweat streamed down his face.

The kind American saw his distress. "Take off your jacket," he suggested.

Matthew shook his head. "I cannot," he said.

"Why not?" the American asked.

Matthew was ashamed to tell the truth. He could only shake his head again.

"Come on," the American urged. "Don't be shy. I'm your friend. My name is Sam."

Still Matthew was ashamed. At last, seeing that Sam was waiting, he unbuttoned his jacket and showed him. He had nothing on underneath.

"I see," Sam said kindly. "It's jacket or nothing. Well, here is something to cool you off—a nice, big dish of ice cream."

He handed the dish to Matthew. On it was a mound of white snow. At least Matthew thought it was snow for he had never seen ice cream. He tasted it. It was not snow. It was sweet and delicious. Sam stood watching and smiling.

It was at this moment, however, that Matthew saw Luke. Luke had eaten his dish of ice cream very quickly, just as quickly as he now took another dish from the table, and he was emptying the ice cream into the pocket of his jacket.

"Luke!" Matthew shouted. "Don't steal!"

Everyone looked at Luke. Matthew was very angry. He went to Luke and put his hand into the pocket to take out the ice cream. He could not. It had melted. He drew out his hand. It was sticky. Sam laughed, and all the men laughed.

"Here," Sam said. "Wipe your hand on this paper napkin."

He held out the paper to Matthew. "What's the matter?" he asked.

For suddenly Matthew was trying not to cry. He had not cried since he was very small and had lost his mother. He had not cried because he knew there was no one to listen. Now he felt helpless. Luke was stealing again. It was too much to bear. All his life suddenly seemed too much for him. He remembered everything at once—the loneliness, the cold winters, the search for work and food, these three boys for whom he was responsible. How could he be responsible for them when Luke was still a thief?

"I'm not really their father," he sobbed.

"Come here with me," Sam said, and he led Matthew aside into a small room. "Now tell me what's wrong," he said.

He sat down and drew Matthew upon his lap. "Tell me everything," he said.

Matthew tried to stop crying so that he could tell Sam everything. But he could not stop at once, and while he sobbed, he felt Sam's arms warm about him. It was the first time he had ever felt arms about him. He stopped crying and looked into Sam's kind blue eyes. Sam was saying something.

"How would you like to be my son?" he was asking.

"Are *you* my father?" he asked.

"No," Sam said, "but I would like to be."

"How can you be my father if you are not?" Matthew asked.

"I could adopt you as my son," Sam said, "and you could adopt me as your father."

Matthew looked at Sam for a minute. He saw a kind face, honest eyes, and a firm mouth. It was an American face. He was half-American himself, and he liked this face.

Then he remembered. "What about Mark, Luke, and John?" he said. "I can't leave them. They wouldn't know what to do without me. I'm their father. They haven't any other."

Sam smiled. "You're much too young to be a father. They really need someone older. Look here, we'll put them in our Company Child Care Center here. They'll have warm clothes, plenty of food, and they can go to school."

Matthew was still troubled. "Luke will not want to go to school."

"Yes, he will," Sam said. "When he finds that he doesn't need to steal because he has food three times a day and he has his own clothes and things, he'll change. We'll see to that."

Every story has its end, and this is the end of Matthew's story, except it is also a beginning. It was the end of living under a bridge, the end of being cold in winter, the end of being hungry. It was the beginning of being the son of Sam and his wife, Ruth.

Of course, Matthew could not know all at once what the new life would mean, a life with a real father and a mother, a life in a new country, where people would be glad he was American, even if he was only half, and where they would not mind that he was also half-Korean. Indeed, they would find that interesting.

He began to understand something about the new life, however, the very day of the Christmas party. For after the party the four boys did not go back to the cave under the bridge. They stayed in the Center, and each of them had a bed to himself and all he could eat. This was change enough, but for Matthew there was a greater change. He began to understand, after a few days, that Sam was more than a kind man. He really wanted to be a father.

Sam came one morning and explained. "You see, Matt, you're my son now. Of course, we'll have to wait for papers to be signed so people will know I'm your father, and Ruth—that's my wife, she's in America—is your mother."

"Does she want to be my mother?" Matthew asked. He had forgotten what it was like to have a mother.

"Oh, indeed she does," Sam said. "I called her on the telephone all the way across the ocean yesterday, and I wish you could have heard how happy her voice was. She said you were the best Christmas gift she could ever have. And she wants you to come quickly."

All this and much more Sam told to Matthew. He came every evening to the Center, and he showed pictures to Matthew, pictures of his new mother, who had a smile on her pretty face, and pictures of his new home that he would soon see.

They talked so often that Matthew began to feel that nothing would be strange to him when he got there, and he was impatient to begin living his new life in America. All except for one thing—he could not stop worrying about Mark, Luke, and John. They seemed to be very happy here in the Center with the other boys, and at first they could not believe he was going to America. America? Where was it? Why did he

want to go there when now he had plenty to eat and warm clothes to wear? These were good arguments, but Matthew wanted more from life. He wanted to be somebody's son. He wanted to have a father and a mother of his own. He tried to explain this to the three boys, but they could not understand.

"Maybe this new father and mother will run away, too," Mark said.

"Sam is not a running-away kind of father," Matthew said, hoping that this was true.

Nevertheless, because of what Mark had said, he was all the more anxious to begin his new life. One day Sam came in very cheerful and very much in a hurry.

"All right, son," he said briskly. "The last paper is signed and delivered and just in time. We're going home, you and I. We leave at noon, so hustle!"

Hustle they did, and they barely had time to buy Matthew a new suit and hurry back to the Center to say goodbye to Mark, Luke, and John. They were in such a hurry that no one had time to feel sad. The three boys could not realize that Matthew was leaving them, nor could he realize it, either. For now he knew that he really was Sam's son. He had wanted to know it before but he did not quite dare, not until he knew he was going to America. Suddenly he also realized he was in a taxicab on his way to the airport, leaving the three boys behind. He grew very silent, so silent that Sam spoke.

"What are you thinking about, son?"

"I'm thinking about Mark, Luke, and John," Matthew said.

He was thinking of how the three boys had looked when he left them at the Center. Everyone had been excited and shouting goodbye and good luck—except Mark, Luke, and John. They were not shouting. They were standing close together, holding hands tightly, as though they were afraid they might lose each other.

"They didn't want me to leave them," Matthew said now in the taxicab.

"Look at me," Sam commanded.,

Matthew obeyed. He looked into Sam's kind blue eyes.

"I want to hear you say 'father,'" Sam said. "'Dad' later, maybe, but now call me your father."

It was true that Matthew had never spoken these words. Why? Because he had not been sure that Sam really would not run away as the other fellows had done. Now he was sure.

"You are my father," he said, and his voice was firm.

Sam could not speak. He just put his arm around Matthew's shoulders.

Matthew knew he would never forget Mark, Luke, and John, but he did not know what to do about them except to remember them. The jet plane carried him across the Pacific Ocean and across the Rocky Mountains, across the plains and rivers until it reached the huge airport in the city of New York.

"Your mother will be waiting for us," Sam told him. "You'll know her when you see her. She's not tall, but short. She has brown hair and brown eyes, and she'll be wearing a red suit of some sort."

"There she is!" Matthew cried.

"Ruth!" Sam shouted.

She came running toward them, and Sam caught her in his arms. For one brief minute Matthew felt shy, but only for one minute. Then she put her arms about him, too.

"Oh, Matthew," she said, "how happy I am that you're our son!"

So Matthew came home at last. There was much for him to discover. He had never lived in a house before, not a house that was also a home. He went up and down stairs many times, just to see what it was like, because he had never lived in a house with stairs. There were all sorts of machines he had never seen before, machines to wash with, to clean with, to look at, to listen to, and he had to learn how to work everything. His father taught him how to play baseball, and then boys came over to play, boys who lived in other houses along the street. He went to school every day and met other children. School was difficult at first because he had never been to school, and he had to begin at the beginning with the smaller children, but he worked hard so that he could catch up with the boys his own age.

Time went fast with so much to learn, and soon it was Christmas again. He had never heard the Christmas story, and his father and mother had to explain it to him. They explained, too, how Christmas happiness overflows into giving gifts.

"Since we cannot give gifts to the Christ Child as the Three Wise Men did on that first Christmas, we give gifts to those we love," his father said.

Matthew planned gifts for his father and mother and each helped him with his gift for the other. Then he had some special friends at school, and he made gifts for them, and his father helped him. And all the time while he did these things he kept thinking about Mark, Luke, and John far away across the sea, and how they had stood holding hands together when he left them. He had never forgotten them, not for a single day. Busy and happy as he had been, he thought of them and was often troubled. Finally, his father, seeing his face sad one night, asked him what was the matter.

Matthew explained and said, "I want to send them a Christmas present."

"Why not?" his father replied.

So Matthew and his father and mother bought new clothes and a toy for each boy and sent them off in time for Christmas.

It was Christmas morning, however, when Matthew put into words something that he had been thinking about for a long time. He had not spoken of it, for he felt it might seem ungrateful, when he had been given so much, to want something more. The gifts this Christmas morning were generous and each was what he had wanted—a small camera, a new sweater, a baseball bat of his own, a ball, books—oh, many things.

"Get everything you want, son?" his father asked.

Matthew nodded. "Thank you," he added. But something in his eyes showed through and his father saw it.

"Come, now," he said. "Tell me what else you want."

"It is not wanting exactly something," Matthew said. His English was good, but he had his own way of talking. "It is something I am still remembering."

"What is it?" his father asked.

"I am remembering last Christmas," Matthew said. "I am remembering Mark, Luke, and John, and how I am their only father."

His father smiled. "It's very well to think of them," he said, "but I still insist that you are too young to be their father."

"I must be their father until they find new fathers," Matthew said.

He thought of last Christmas and all the change in his life. Were they happy, those children to whom he had promised to be a father?

"Well, then," his father was saying. "We'll have to try to find some new fathers for them, eh, Ruth?"

His mother was looking at Matthew, her eyes tender with sudden tears. "I am sure we can find some fathers for them," she said, "and mothers to go with the fathers. Fathers alone are not quite enough."

"Hear that, Matt?" his father said. "You can't be father and mother, too, and they'll need both."

"On this street," his mother said, "there are many fathers and mothers. If we told them about Mark, Luke, and John—"

His father interrupted. "There'd be more than enough to go around. Of course, there will be some fathers and mothers who won't want to go through all that paperwork I had to go through for you, Matt."

"There'll certainly be three couples who will think it was all worthwhile, just as we do," his mother said.

This was the way it was on that Christmas day. Once they had decided, his father and mother began making telephone calls. People came into the house that evening, and while the Christmas tree was bright with many lights, Matthew told them about Mark, Luke, and John. He told them everything, how at first he had lived alone under the bridge, and how, one after the other, he had found Mark, Luke, and John.

"That was how I became their father," he said at last. "And now I would like to find new fathers for them, because I can't be a mother, too, and each boy needs two people, father and mother."

The people listened, smiling, even laughing when they heard how Luke had put ice cream into his pocket, but at the end they were not laughing. Some of them were wiping tears from their eyes.

"How about it, neighbors?" Sam asked.

That was how it began, but it would not be finished in a day, nor even in a few days.

"We can't expect that, though, can we, son?" Sam said. "Remember how long you had to wait for me to get all the papers signed and finished? And you waited, didn't you? Well, Mark, Luke, and John must wait, too. But just remember that it wasn't only you who waited. I waited, and so did your mother; and we were impatient, I can tell you, but we had to wait. So while Mark, Luke, and John wait over there, just remember their new fathers and mothers are waiting here."

"Will Mark, Luke, and John be here before next Christmas?" Matthew asked.

"Oh, yes," his mother said, "long, long before next Christmas."

"Then that will be the happiest Christmas of all," Matthew said.

It was the end of the day, a happy Christmas day. Suddenly he was sleepy. So much had happened, and he did not need to worry anymore about Mark, Luke, and John. He was not their father now, just their friend.

"Good night, dear Father and Mother," he said, "and thank you."

He let them kiss him for once, although he was really too big for kisses, he thought, but they were good to him and his heart overflowed. He went upstairs, and suddenly he had a new feeling. All this time he had been too shy to sing even the Christmas carols, but now, without thinking, he opened his mouth and his voice came out loud and clear.

"Joy to the world," he sang.

Downstairs, Sam and Ruth, hearing that young joyous voice, looked at each other and smiled as only a man and woman can smile at each other when they share a child.

Their Best Christmas

Hartley F. Dailey

John and Mary Channing looked out at the falling snow with understandable bitterness. It was Christmas—and none of their children were coming home, not even those who lived only minutes away.

Suddenly there was a knock on the door. Who could that be? They had seen no car come up the drive.

Hartley F. Dailey, writing from Springfield, Ohio, has become one of the most beloved contributors to this series, author of such favorites as "Joey's Miracle," "Yet Not One of Them Shall Fall," and "The Red Mittens."

John Channing looked out the dining room window to where the snow drifted deeper and deeper across his front yard. It was snowing so hard now that the woodlot, only 50 yards away, was only a gray blur. A big drift ran from the corner of the house, diagonally across the drive, to join the one that reached out from the grape arbor.

"Christmas!" said John. He almost spat the word.

Mary, his wife, looked up from where she was setting the table, startled and a little concerned at the bitterness in his voice. "Don't take it so hard, John," she admonished him gently.

He turned from the window to face her, "But Mother, what kind of Christmas is it, all by ourselves? Four kids and a flock of grandchildren, and we have to eat Christmas dinner all alone!"

"Now, Dad," her voice was even more gentle. "You know Molly couldn't leave her job in the store during Christmas. If she did, there'd be no job, and *then* how could she finish college?"

"I know all that." He came over and put his arm around her. "I know Leah can't get home, either, what with living 600 miles away, and her children in school, and Tom's job to think of. But the other two, I find it hard to understand. Debbie's just five miles away, and Bill only seven. So busy with their own affairs they can't even spend a couple hours with us on Christmas."

"But John, the weather—"

"*Bother* the weather!" He was angry again. "You know very well they told us they wouldn't be here, even before this blizzard blew up."

"Yes, I know." Her voice was sad, and somehow tired. "But maybe they'll understand some day. No use fretting, I guess. Come, help me carry in the food, then we'll sit down and eat. At least," she added, "they sent presents."

"Presents!" He looked toward the foot of the tree where the gifts were laid out on the floor, things that he had desired and would later cherish. But just now they might as well be heaps of ashes.

He helped her carry in the food—a very small chicken, a single pumpkin pie, minimal servings of

other dishes. And he knew that even these would not all be eaten. Then just as they were sitting down, there was a knock at the kitchen door. He opened the door to find a man standing there—a man who was small, young, and timid, and very obviously not dressed for such weather. He was covered from head to foot with crusted snow and breathing so hard he had to make several attempts before he could utter a sound.

"Please, mister," he managed at last, "could you help me? It's my car. It went off the road, must be a mile and a half back."

"Come in, sir!" John opened the door wide. "Now, catch your breath and tell me all about it. Where did it happen?"

"Back that way," the man gestured vaguely. "There's a funny bend in the road. I—I couldn't see where I was going, the snow was so bad. Then all at once it was too late."

"Devil's Neck," John growled. "Happens all the time. Anyone else in the car?"

"My wife and children," the stranger told him. "I had to leave them there. They couldn't have made it in the snow. I walked and walked, looking for a house. Doesn't anybody live along here?"

"For land's sake, come on, friend," John was already putting on his boots. "We'll have to get them out of there. They'll freeze!" Then in a more gentle tone, he added, "There's two other houses, but they're set way back. You couldn't have seen them for the snow."

"Mother," he called, as he put on his coat, "fix up some more food, a lot of it. We're having guests to dinner. Hungry ones. There won't be time to cook more chicken or turkey, but you can fry up a bunch of burgers, and put some of your frozen pies in the oven. Oh, what in the world am I telling *you* for? You know better what to do than I do!" His voice sounded years younger than it had 20 minutes earlier.

As they backed out of the garage, the young man asked, "Aren't you afraid you'll hang up in the snow, too?"

"Not a bit," John chuckled. "I'm prepared. Chains."

The stranger's family, besides his wife, consisted of four children, the oldest about 9, the youngest about 16 months. They bundled them quickly into John's car, but John shook his head sadly over the condition of the other vehicle. It was deep in the ditch, far off the road, and the drift was rapidly building up around it.

"Take a tractor and some shovels to get that out," he said. "Best thing to do now is get these youngsters home. Nobody's going to bother the car here. We'll come back for it after we eat."

The big farm kitchen was fragrant with the smell of cooking meat, together with the spicy odor of mince and pumpkin pies. Mary met them at the door, helping the children out of their too-thin wraps, showing each one where to stand to get maximum heat from the furnace, taking the smallest one up in her arms, exclaiming over her silky brown hair.

"Just like Molly's used to be."

"I think we'd better introduce ourselves," the young man shyly broke in. "I'm George Lewis. We've been living in Chicago, but I lost my job, and we're going to a job I have been promised down in Tennessee. My wife is Vera. This"—indicating the eldest girl—"is Sally.

The middle one is Marty, and the baby is Lora. This big fellow is my son, Bob."

John Channing, reaching gravely to shake hands with the 6-year-old, found himself looking into a pair of serious gray eyes that might have belonged to his own son, 18 years before.

"Dinner's ready, John," Mary announced. "Don't let's stand around chinning. These children must be hungry!"

The big dining table was loaded to capacity. John had never ceased to marvel at his wife's ability to prepare a good meal in a hurry. There was a huge platter of burgers, of course, and, amazingly, a great bowl of mashed potatoes. How *had* she managed those in such a short time? There were pies and cranberry sauce, peas, corn, and lima beans, that had come from their well-stocked freezer. Yes, and pickles, relish, and jellies, that Mary had canned last summer. It did his heart good to see the children's eyes bulge at the sight of all that food. He was ready to bet they hadn't sat down to such a feast in many a day.

"We're just farmers here," he chuckled. "There's nothing rich or fancy about us, but we eat well. Yes, sir, we eat well!"

Then as they became quiet, he bowed his head to ask a blessing. "Dear God," he prayed, "we thank Thee for this day on which we celebrate the beginning of the greatest sacrifice. We thank Thee for continued health and for the food Thou has supplied in such abundance. But most of all, we thank Thee for these unexpected guests, who have come to brighten the bleakness of our day. Wilt Thou go with them and prosper them in their new home. All this we ask in His dear Name, amen."

During the meal Mrs. Lewis explained further about their reason for being stranded. "George is a pressman," she began in her soft southern voice. "He was working for a publishing company in Chicago. We'd bought a home there. We were doing pretty well.

"But something went wrong, bad management, I guess. Anyway, the company went out of business, and George was out of work. He couldn't find another position. The publishing business really isn't what it used to be. His unemployment insurance ran out. He had some life insurance, and we borrowed all we could on that. And then, I had appendicitis and had to have an operation.

"We were at wit's end, when my father wrote that he had a job for George on a newspaper down near home. We'd sold our house and used our equity to pay our bills, so all we had to do was to pile into the car and start out. If it hadn't been for this storm, we'd have been there tonight."

After the meal, John and George took the tractor, a log chain, and some shovels and set out to get the stranded car. But they found this no small task. The car was all but buried in drifts, and the tractor wheels found poor footing on the snow-covered road. It took hours of shoveling, hitching and re-hitching, to get it on the road again. It was dark when they got back to the farmhouse. The Lewises wanted to push on at once, but the Channings wouldn't permit it.

"Nonsense!" said John. "The snow hasn't stopped falling yet, and they have hardly begun to clear the roads. You wouldn't go five miles till you'd be stranded again. You'll stay here tonight and go on tomorrow, when the going will be better."

"If you'd like," he addressed George, "you can help me do my feeding. It's way past time now."

After a late supper, they were listening as Marty, the 4-year-old, recounted her version of the journey. "An' we stayed all night in a mo-tel," she piped, "an' Santy Claus never comed at all. I guess he jus' couldn't find us."

John took his wife aside. "You've got a bunch of Molly's old things in the attic," he said. "I think there's even some toys. Why don't we—"

"But John—" she interrupted.

There was a trace of bitterness in his voice again as he said, "Yes, I know, you won't part with them, because they're Molly's. Has Molly ever looked at them in recent years? Does she even know they're there—or care? Why not get some good out of them?"

In the end, Mary was quite as happy as he to bring down the big box of clothes from the attic and pick out things for each of the girls. She even managed to find a little leather jacket for Bobby, one that had belonged to Bill years ago. It was a little large, perhaps, but it would keep him warm, and he'd grow into it.

When Mary began to pass out dolls to the little girls, John went out to the garage to get the baseball bat and glove his son had once loved with unbelievable passion, though John would never admit the twinge it gave his own heart to part with them. When he came back, he found Mary crying softly over the picture little Lora made in a little velvet dress and fur trimmed coat that had once been Molly's.

Sally, in a coat that had also been Molly's not too many years before, pirouetted in front of her Mother.

"You know, Mommy," she beamed, "this is just about the best Christmas we ever had!"

Some time later, John himself echoed almost those very words. He was standing in the middle of the bedroom, winding his alarm clock. He was dead tired, and his muscles ached from long hours of unaccustomed work in the cold and snow. But for the first time in years, every bed in the big old house was full, and he would long remember the shining eyes and laughing voices of those children.

"You know, Mary," he mused, "this was just about the nicest Christmas we ever had."

And his wife, already in bed before him, murmured sleepily, "Yes, John, I *do* believe it was."

A Stolen Christmas

Charles M. Sheldon

Christmas for the Gray family no longer held any surprises—everyone knew ahead of time what each would receive. And each year, the amount of money paid for these gifts continued to escalate. Affluence had taken all the joy out of Christmas.

This year was just as bad or worse—until the unexpected happened.

Dr. Charles M. Sheldon (1857-1946), Congregational minister, and editor of Christian Herald *(1920-1925), is best known for his landmark book,* In His Steps, *which has become one of the best-sellers of all time. Sheldon was in the forefront of the Social Gospel movement, and believed that doctrine and legalism were most inadequate substitutions for really living one's faith and exhibiting Christlike caring, on a day-by-day basis, for the Lord's sheep.*

Careful now, John," said Mrs. Mary Gray, as her big, tall husband stood on tiptoe and leaned over to fasten a small object on the very top of the Christmas tree.

The object was a gilt paper angel, blowing a silver trumpet on which were the words, "Glory to God in the highest!"

John fastened it securely, after several trials. After descending the ladder and stepping back, he gave a deep sigh, and said, "How do you like it, Mary?"

"Lovely! Beautiful! Splendid!" said Mary, using up three of her best adjectives at once.

"Well, I hope it will do," replied John soberly.

"Of course, it will do. What makes you talk so!" said Mary with a tone of reproach.

"Well, you know it is so different from what it used to be. There are no happy surprises for the children any more. Rob has been teasing for that gun for two months, and he knows he is going to get it. And Dorothy picked out that speaking doll two weeks ago, and she knows what it is. And Paul opened the package containing his automobile when it came up the other day. There's not much fun getting Christmas presents anymore. It's an old story by the time you have them."

"You old growler," said Mary. "You are tired. Let's go into the library and rest. The tree itself will be a surprise, won't it? The children don't know about *that*."

"I hope not," replied John as they went out and shut the door.

They passed through the sitting room into the library and sat down on opposite sides of a reading table. Mrs. Gray looked a little anxiously at her husband.

"You don't begrudge the work of giving the children a happy time at Christmas, do you, John?"

"Of course not. You wouldn't think so if you saw me getting that tree. I wanted one thing that I got myself, instead of buying it, and you know what a job I had getting it from Fisher's Cove. I believe the children will be surprised when they see it. But it doesn't seem quite natural to light it up in the morning."

"We must, though. We promised them their presents in the morning. You're sure you didn't forget anything?"

"Pretty sure," replied John gravely. "Want me to go over the list? High-class repeating rifle for Rob. Automatic speaking, singing, and walking doll for Dorothy. Real gasoline toy engine automobile for Paul. Two pounds of assorted candy for each. Then there is the warship, exact copy of the *Kansas*, with real guns and powder, for Rob and Paul together. Football and headgear for Rob. Reflectoscope for Paul. Card case for Dorothy, and two bottles of perfume. *The Bandit of the Sierras* for Paul. Complete china tea set for Dorothy, with electric lamps for the table. Besides what you hung up for me and what I hung up for you."

"John," said Mary coaxingly, "what was that queer-looking bundle you hung on the big limb near the window? Was that for me?"

"You're as bad as the children," said John, laughing. "What do you want to know for?"

"I can't wait till morning, John; *tell* me."

"No, ma'am. I won't do it. Can't you wait a few hours? It's almost 11:00 now. The children will be awake in six hours, and we will all come down together. That's the plan, isn't it?"

"Yes. Oh, well, I can wait. It's something pretty, I hope."

"I hope it is," said John anxiously.

"Because, John, you remember last Christmas you got me that patented dishwasher that broke everything into bits when you turned the handle."

"That was because I read the directions wrong and turned the thing backward," said John hastily.

"Well, I hope you have got me something lovely this time. I have yours."

"What is it, Mary? *Tell* me."

"You're as bad as I am. No, sir. You'll have to wait. There's one thing I feel sorry about, though; I wish you hadn't got that gun for Rob. I'm in mortal terror he will shoot himself or somebody else."

"Of course not. If he is going to be an American citizen he has got to learn how to handle firearms. He may be a brigadier general or an admiral someday."

"I hope not, John. Besides, I have been wondering a little lately if guns and warships are appropriate Christmas presents."

"Oh, pshaw, Mary! Anything is appropriate if you have the money to get it. The main thing about Christmas time is getting something. The bother is to know what to get. The gun won't hurt Rob any more than the candy."

"You got too much of that. Just think, John, two pounds apiece. And Uncle Terry always sends in such a lot of candy every Christmas."

"Oh, well, we can give some of it to Lizzie. She never has enough. Or else send it out to the poor farm."

"Yes, that's what we will do," declared Mary.

81

CIMH6-6

"Well," said John, as he rose, yawning, "let's have one more look at the tree before we go up."

He and his wife went to the door and opened it. John turned on the electric lights, and he and Mary stepped into the room.

At first, they could not grasp the obvious fact. John rubbed his eyes and opened them again. Mary ran forward with a sudden cry, and then stood in the middle of the room.

The Christmas tree was *gone*, along with everything that had been hung on it and placed at its foot! Not a thing was left except a few broken strings of popcorn, two or three wax candles, a shred or two of gaudy tinsel and bits of evergreen. The tree itself was simply gone.

Mary ran forward to the big window that opened on the side veranda. It stood wide open, and other fragments of the tree and its trimmings were littered on the broad window sill. In the middle of the sill, resting calmly on its side, was the gilt paper angel and its trumpet, the only thing left behind intact.

"John, oh, John, someone has stolen our tree!" cried Mary as the full enormity of the event became clear. She ran to the open window, but John was there before her. He leaped out upon the veranda. Bits of evergreen and small strings of popcorn showed which way the thief, or thieves, had gone, straight across the lawn, out to the middle of the road, and there the trail ceased.

"They had a wagon!" gasped John.

Mary had followed to the edge of the curb. "Quick, John! Run in and telephone the police station. They may catch them yet. Oh, to think of our Christmas—"

John was already in the house, snatching up the receiver.

Did you ever have to telephone to a fire station that your house was afire and you wanted the department to hurry up before the house was burned to the ground? Then you can sympathize with John Gray on this Christmas Eve as he waited what seemed to him like a whole hour before he heard a lazy voice say, "Yes, this is the police station."

"Say! Send a man or two out here quick. Someone has stolen our Christmas."

"What!"

"Send someone right out here quick. Our Christmas has been robbed, stolen, do you hear?"

"Yes. Stolen! What has been stolen?"

"Christmas!"

"Christmas *what!*"

"Oh, John!" broke in Mary, wringing her hands and crying hysterically. "Tell the man it is our tree—our *tree!* Our Christmas tree is gone."

"Tree!" roared John. "Christmas tree. Someone has stolen our Christmas tree. Do you get that?"

"Free?" came over the wire.

"No. Tree! Tree! Christmas tree! Send someone right out here, will you?"

"Out where?"

"Out *here!*"

"Where is it?"

"Oh, give him the name and number, John!" Mary cried again.

"John Gray. 719 Plymouth Avenue. Come quick, won't you?"

"All right. Be out there with the patrol."

John hung up the receiver and turned to Mary. She had sunk into a chair and was sobbing. At the sight, John began to recover some of his wits.

"Don't cry, Mary. The police will get them. They can't have had much of a start."

"But who would steal a Christmas tree? It might be some prank of the Raymond boys."

"No, I don't believe they would do that. Besides, you know Raymond never lets them stay out after 9:00, and here it is nearly midnight."

"What shall we *do*? How can we keep Christmas? To think of all those presents—" Mary broke down again at the thought.

"I hope the six-shooter and the warship will go off at the same time and kill 'em," muttered John darkly.

"And there was your present to me," said Mary with a groan. "Now I shall never get it."

"Maybe you will. I can get another."

"Oh, why couldn't you go downtown and buy some more things?" cried Mary suddenly.

"Too late," John replied gloomily. "Besides, the stores are all closing up. And besides, I haven't the money to buy any more six-shooters and real toy automobiles."

"But what will the children do?" asked Mary desperately. "Here we are without a single thing for them. It will break their hearts to have a Christmas and no presents."

"Maybe we could borrow a few of the Morgans'. They always have stacks more than they need."

Mary was about to reply indignantly to this levity on John's part when the patrol car arrived. Two officers came in, and John and Mary answered questions and

showed them the place where the tree had stood, and where they were sitting when it was stolen, and where all traces of it had ceased in the road.

After the officers had examined all the evidence and had departed, after solemn promises to do all in their power to catch the thieves, John and Mary heard the clock strike the half hour.

"We shall never see that tree again," declared Mary in resignation. "Now what shall we do? We must have *something* for the children. I am going to make some candy."

"It's past midnight," objected John.

"I don't care. I can make some from mother's recipe, in the chafing dish."

Mary went out into the kitchen, and John, after standing irresolute for a minute, went upstairs. He peeped into the boys' bedroom as he turned on the hall light. They were sleeping peacefully, and on Rob's placid face there was anything but the warlike look of a brigadier general or an admiral.

Mr. Gray turned out the light and went on up another flight of stairs to his den. He sat down at an old desk, pulled out various drawers, and took out half a dozen articles, wrapping each one carefully, and marking them with the children's names. He gathered them up and came downstairs.

Mary was busy over the chafing dish.

"I've thought of a plan," said John, spreading out the articles on the table. "You put the candy in their stockings, and one of these in each. Then we'll hide the rest somewhere and ask them to find them after dinner. There's that Chinese god Colfax sent me last year from Tientsin, and the little box of Japanese water flowers that has never been opened, and the fairytales Graves sent us from Tokyo. I've been keeping them for rainy days, and the children have never seen them."

"Just the thing!" exclaimed Mary with enthusiasm. "Oh, John, you are the brightest man—except when at the telephone. I never knew you to get a message straight yet. But what shall we tell the children about the tree?"

"Tell them the truth," said John wisely. "The excitement will keep them from thinking about their loss."

That was the strangest Christmas the Gray family had ever spent. Before 5:00, three children were sitting up wide awake.

Rob whispered to his brother. "I know what they've got. A tree. Father tried to sneak it into the barn two nights ago, but I saw him. Let's go down and turn on the light before Father and Mother wake up. I want to see my gun."

"And I want to start my automobile," said Paul, hastily climbing out of bed.

"And I want to wind up my doll and hear it cry," said Dorothy.

The three white figures stole downstairs with no more noise than that made by Rob as he fell over a rug in the hall.

They opened the door in the parlor and turned on the light and stared. Instead of a beautiful tree, they saw the well-known furniture of the room and nothing else, except three stockings hanging from the parlor mantel.

Their astonished exclamations awakened their parents. When they came down, the matter was explained. The boys looked very sober. But as the family sat down to breakfast, Dorothy relieved the seriousness by leaving her place, going over to her father, and saying, "What if those wicked men had shot you and Mother. That would have been even worse, wouldn't it?"

"I believe it would, for *us*," said John Gray with a laugh that changed into a half-sob when Dorothy put her arms around his neck and kissed him.

They were all at breakfast when their nearest neighbor, Mark Raymond, came in. "Just read about your loss in the paper! It's the meanest thing I ever heard of. But I've found one of the things. I was out early and saw this bundle lying close in by the curb in front of my house, and it has your name written on it, Mrs. Gray."

"Oh, my present!" exclaimed Mary. It was the queer-shaped package she had asked John about. She hastily cut the string and unwrapped the package. "What is it?" she said when it was uncovered.

"It's a combination towel rack and shaving mirror and—"

But that was about as far as John got. Everybody roared, Mark Raymond with the rest. Rob got hold of the combination and tried to work it, and something caught his fingers and pinched them. They all roared again—except Rob. Mary laughed until she cried. When they could not laugh anymore, Mark Raymond rose to go.

"Well, no use to wish you folks a Merry Christmas. You seem to be having one all right."

"We've got one another," said Mary, looking mischievously at John. "I don't believe any other man in town would buy his wife a towel rack and shaving mirror combined."

John looked a little disturbed at first, then his face cleared up. "You see, Raymond, my wife is different from all the rest. She can take a joke even when it isn't meant."

Raymond looked at Gray with hesitation. Then he spoke suddenly. "Say, Gray, can you—would you and Mrs. Gray go to church this morning, if you had an invitation?"

"Church?"

"Yes. You see, I belong to the Brotherhood at church. You know Reverend Strong. Well, he is holding a Christmas morning service. Lots of good music and a short sermon. Mr. Vinge plays the organ. The English have Christmas Day services in their churches and everybody goes."

John Gray looked undecided. "Oh, I don't know. I'm not much of a churchgoer, as you know, Raymond."

"That's the reason I'm asking you," said Raymond with a smile. "Be delighted to have you come. Both of you."

"Why not?" said Mrs. Gray. "Lizzie will get dinner. No one has stolen our turkey. I saw it go into the oven. And I like to hear Strong."

Rob spoke eagerly. "Did you say Mr. Vinge is going to play the organ?"

"Yes," said Raymond.

"I want to hear him," said Rob, who was music-loving in spite of his warlike proclivities. "Can't I go?"

"Me, too," chimed in Paul.

"I won't stay here alone. I want to go too," said Dorothy.

"We'll all go," said Mary decidedly.

"I don't care," laughed John. "It's a queer Christmas

to start with and might as well be queer to go on with. I never went to church on Christmas in my life."

"Won't hurt you," said Raymond much pleased. "Sit with my folks. We are all going."

So an hour later John Gray and his wife and their children were in church with their neighbors, the Raymonds. John felt a little bewildered. But he had been more or less bewildered ever since he opened the parlor door to find the Christmas tree stolen. As the service went on, the beauty of it crept in upon him. The church was trimmed with wreaths, and up near the pulpit was a tree, shapely and benignant, with no presents on it, but lighted with small electric lamps, and tinged with white. Vinge, the blind organist, sat at his beloved instrument. What melody flowed out of it! The Christmas glory flooded his keys.

John glanced at his wife. Her face was wrapped with tender feeling. "Glory to God in the Highest," sang the children's choir. The fresh young voices were fragrant of Bethlehem and the Nativity. Gray looked along at his children. Rob, the warlike, was lost to all the world, his boyish face upturned to catch all sound, his eyes fixed on Vinge, his soul caught in the meshes of that blind man's harmony. Something choked John Gray. What if sometime his boy should be a great organ player! What fine children God had given him!

His glance came back to his wife. What a lovely face she had. What a beautiful mother she had always been. How devoted to her husband. How proud of him, in spite of his awkward blunders and many faults. He quietly reached for her hand and thrilled at the clasp of her warm, firm fingers. She smiled at him, and then together

they listened to Phillips Brooks' most beautiful hymn, "O little town of Bethlehem/How still we see thee lie." A little later in the service they joined their voices with the congregation, as they sang "Angels from the realms of glory/Wing your flight o'er all the earth."

Then the sermon touched them. Even the children could understand it, it was so simple, and so clear in telling what Christ meant to the earth.

When the service closed in a quiet moment of worship, the people rose silently and went out. At the door, Gray exchanged greetings with several friends, and as he walked along home, he said to his wife, "Say, Mary, I liked that. Wonder why the churches in America don't have Christmas Day services more generally."

"It meant more to me than I can tell, John. Somehow I feel younger and happier. Doesn't that seem queer, when all our presents were stolen, except mine?"

They both laughed.

"We have each other," said John gently.

"And the children," said Mary.

"And the children," John agreed.

After dinner, the children hunted for the other articles their father had hidden. They were simple things, saved for rainy-day use, but they were real surprises. Near the big window in search of her present, Dorothy discovered the gilt angel with the trumpet. It had lain peacefully there during all the excitement.

Mrs. Gray put it on the mantel over the clock. Later in the day, while the children were out in the kitchen cracking some nuts Rob had stored in the barn last fall, she said to John, "I believe that angel has something to do with our happiness. Doesn't it seem strange to you, John?

It was a dreadful loss, but we don't seem to be feeling so dreadful about it. After all, the boys never got the gun or the warship. And they don't seem to feel so very bad."

A shout of laughter came from the kitchen where some of the Raymond children were visiting with the Grays and showing them their presents. And they could hear Dorothy say in a tone of superiority, "But that's nothing. We had a *burglar* in our house last night!"

"It does seem strange," said John. "The police just phoned that they can get no clue to the robbery. It's been a very different sort of Christmas. Mary, what were you going to give me in exchange for the towel rack?"

"Go up to your den and find it," said Mary shyly.

John went up, two steps at a time. On his writing desk he found it—a photograph of his wife, framed in an old-gold oval frame that had belonged to her mother.

When he came down, he was met by Mary at the foot of the stairs.

"Oh, John, do you like it? And it's a surprise to me, too. I thought it was gone with the rest. But when you went through the window, I saw my present to you on the veranda, and saved it for a surprise. Do you know another woman in town who wouldn't have told?"

"No, I don't. And I don't know another like you in any way." And John kissed his wife, who actually blushed for happiness.

Later in the evening, as the family sat in front of the fire eating nuts and apples, Mrs. Gray asked Dorothy to go into the library and bring a box she would find on the big table. When it was brought in, Mrs. Gray asked Dorothy to open it. Faded tissue paper wrappings came off. And there lay an old-fashioned doll, dressed in India muslin, with quaint ribbons under a Converse hat. Dorothy was overcome.

Mary whispered to John, "Bessie's doll. I haven't had the heart to give it to anyone until today."

A tear fell on John's hand as the memory of their first child crept into the firelight and softened the glow of that new Christmas. Later, when the children were asleep, Dorothy, hugging the India muslin doll up to her cheek, John and Mary came down and sat by the fire.

"After all, we have had a beautiful day, Mary," John said. "We have one another."

"And the children," said Mary.

And the firelight flung a flame a little higher than the rest so that the trumpet of the gilt angel stood out very clear with the words, "Glory to God in the highest and on earth peace among men in whom he is well pleased."

Then there stole into the hearts of John Gray and Mary Gray, his wife, at the close of that blessed Christmas Day, something more like the Peace of God than they had ever known. The Christ Child meant more to them than He had ever meant. And in their hearts they both yearned for a better life, glorified by Him who is the peace of those whose hearts are restless, and the joy of those whose hearts are sad.

To See Again

Gary B. Swanson

We all take our senses for granted, placing, instead, undue value on monetary things. We'd be happy, we say, if Publisher's Clearing House made us multimillionaires. But multimillionaires are rarely very happy, so there must be something wrong with that assertion. This little story reminds us that there are some things that dwarf mere money.

Gary Swanson, of Columbia, Maryland, has taught both on the high school and college levels, has been in public relations, has edited such publications as Listen *magazine,* Collegiate Quarterly, *and* Cornerstone Connections, *and has written about a thousand poems, essays, and short stories. This particular story is true and took place in central California a number of years ago.*

The mother sat on the simulated-leather chair in the doctor's office, picking nervously at her fingernail. Wrinkles of worry lined her forehead as she watched 5-year-old Kenny sitting on the rug before her.

He was small for his age and a little too thin, she thought. His fine blond hair hung down smooth and straight to the top of his ears. But white gauze bandages encircled his head, covering his eyes and pinning his ears back.

In his lap he bounced a beaten-up teddy bear. It was the pride of his life, yet one arm was gone and one eye missing. Twice his mother had tried to throw it away, to replace it with a new one, but he had fussed so much she had relented. She tipped her head slightly to the side and smiled at him. *It's really about all he has,* she sighed to herself.

A nurse appeared in the doorway. "Kenny Ellis," she announced, and the young mother scooped the boy up and followed the nurse toward the examination room. The hallway smelled of rubbing alcohol and bandages. Children's crayon drawings lined the walls.

"The doctor will be with you in a moment," the nurse said with an efficient smile. "Please be seated."

The mother placed Kenny on the examination table. "Be careful, honey, not to fall off."

"Am I up very high, Mother?"

"No, dear, but be careful."

Kenny hugged his teddy bear tighter. "Then I don't want Grr-face to fall either."

The mother smiled. The smile twisted at the corners into a frown of concern. She brushed the hair out of the boy's face and caressed his cheek, soft as thistledown, with the back of her hand. As the office music drifted into a haunting version of "Silent Night," she remembered the accident for the thousandth time.

She had been cooking things on the back burners for years. But there it was, sitting right out in front, the water almost boiling for oatmeal.

The phone rang in the living room. It was another one of those "free offers" that cost so much. At the very moment she returned the phone to the table, Kenny

screamed in the kitchen, the galvanizing cry of pain that frosts a mother's veins.

She winced again at the memory of it and brushed aside a warm tear slipping down her cheek. Six weeks they had waited for this day to come. "We'll be able to take the bandages off the week before Christmas," the doctor had said.

The door to the examination room swept open, and Dr. Harris came in. "Good morning, Mrs. Ellis," he said brightly. "How are you today?"

"Fine, thank you," she said. But she was too apprehensive for small talk.

Dr. Harris bent over the sink and washed his hands carefully. He was cautious with his patients but careless about himself. He could seldom find time to get a haircut, and his straight black hair hung a little long over his collar. His loosened tie allowed his collar to be open at the throat.

"Now, then," he said, sitting down on a stool, "let's have a look."

Gently he snipped at the bandage with scissors and unwound it from Kenny's head. The bandage fell away, leaving two flat squares of gauze taped directly over Kenny's eyes. Dr. Harris lifted the edges of the tape slowly, trying not to hurt the boy's tender skin.

Kenny slowly opened his eyes and blinked several times as if the sudden light hurt. Then he looked at his mother and grinned. "Hi, Mom," he said.

Choking and speechless, the mother threw her arms around Kenny's neck. For several minutes she could say nothing as she hugged the boy and wept in thankfulness. Finally, she looked at Dr. Harris with tear-filled eyes. "I don't know how we'll ever be able to pay you," she said. "Since my husband died it's been hard for us."

"We've been over all that before," the doctor interrupted with a wave of his hand. "I know how things are for you and Kenny. I'm glad I could help."

The mother dabbed at her eyes with a well-used handkerchief, stood up, and took Kenny's hand. But just as she turned toward the door Kenny pulled away and stood for a long moment looking uncertainly at the doctor. Then he held his teddy bear up by its one arm to the doctor.

"Here," he said, "take my Grr-face. He ought to be worth a lot of money."

Dr. Harris quietly took the broken bear in his two hands. "Thank you, Kenny. This will more than pay for my services."

The last few days before Christmas were especially good for Kenny and his mother. They sat together in the long evenings, watching the Christmas tree lights twinkle on and off. Bandages had covered Kenny's eyes for six weeks, so he seemed reluctant to close them in sleep at night. The fire dancing in the fireplace, the snowflakes sticking to his bedroom window, the two small packages under the tree—all the lights and colors of the holiday fascinated him.

And then, on Christmas Eve, Kenny's mother answered the doorbell. No one was there, but a large box was on the porch, wrapped in metallic green paper with a broad red ribbon and bow. A tag attached to the bow identified the box as intended for Kenny Ellis.

With a grin, Kenny tore the ribbon off the box, lifted the lid, and pulled out a teddy bear—his beloved

Grr-face. Only it now had a new arm of brown corduroy and two new button eyes that glittered in the soft Christmas light. Kenny didn't seem to mind that the new arm did not match the other one. He just hugged his teddy bear and laughed.

Among the tissue in the box, the mother found a card. "Dear Kenny," it read, "I can sometimes help put boys and girls back together, but Mrs. Harris had to help me repair Grr-face. She's a better bear doctor than I am. Merry Christmas! Dr. Harris."

"Look, Mother," Kenny smiled, pointing to the button eyes. "Grr-face can see again—just like me!"

Bid the Tapers Twinkle

Bess Streeter Aldrich

When you have grown old, about all you have left, sometimes, is family. In the case of old Mrs. Atkin there was not even that, for this Christmas not one of that big crowd was coming home for Christmas. She just didn't see how she could make it through.

Bess Streeter Aldrich (1881-1954), author of "Star Across the Tracks" in Christmas in My Heart, *book 3, wrote about the Midwest frontier in a loving yet realistic manner. Some of her most famous books include* Lantern in Her Hand, A White Bird Flying, The Rim of the Prairie, *and* Spring Came On Forever. *Her typical work encapsulates life in its entirety (from childhood to old age), and she maintains that love, marriage, and children are the most important things in life.*

The Atkin house sat well back in a tree-filled yard on a busy corner of town, its wide frame porch running around two sides, 30 feet of it facing Churchill Avenue, 30 feet facing Seventh Street, its long brick walk sloping across the lot to an iron gateway in the exact corner, as though with impartial deference to both streets.

The arrangement might have been almost symbolic of the character of old Mrs. Atkin, who had lived there for many years, so impartially gracious to her well-to-do Churchill Avenue callers and her hired help from Seventh Street.

Old Sara Atkin had known the town longer than anyone now living in it. Indeed, she had arrived as a bride only a few weeks after the first timbers were laid for the sawmill which became the nucleus of a village. She had seen a store go up near the sawmill, a single pine room with a porch across the front, onto which a man threw a sack of mail from the back of a pony twice a week. She had seen the first house built—a queer little box of a cottonwood house; had seen another follow, and others; then a one-roomed schoolhouse and a stout frame church with a thick spire like a work-worn hand pointing a clumsy finger to the blue sky. She had seen whips of cottonwood trees set out at the edge of the grassy streets, had watched them grow to giants, live out their lives and fall to the ground under the axes of the third generation. She had seen a shining roadway of steel laid through the village and the first iron horse snort its way into the sunset. All these things and many others had old Sara Atkin seen.

John Atkin had gone back to Ohio for her and brought her by wagon and ferry to his bachelor sod house on land he had purchased from the railroad company for two dollars an acre. She had been 19 then, her cheeks as pink as the wild roses that sprang up in the prairie grass, her eyes as blue as the wild gentians that grew near them.

A few years later they had moved into a new three-room house with a lean-to and turned the soddie over to the stock. John Atkin had possessed the knack of making money where some of his neighbors had not. He had started a general store and a sorghum mill, had shipped in coal and lumber, had prospered to such an extent in a short time, that they were able to build the present residence, a castle of a house for the raw prairie town—so unusual, with its parlor and back parlor and its two fireplaces, that people had driven for miles in their top buggies or buckboards to see its capacious framework and the mottled marble of its mantels.

When it was completed, new furniture had come for it too—walnut bedsteads and center tables and a tall hall rack with a beveled-glass mirror. But the house which had once been such a source of pride to the whole community was merely a fussy and rather shabby old place now, with its furniture outmoded. John Atkin had been dead for many years, and Sara, whose cheeks had once been like wild roses, was a great-grandmother.

In the passing years the town had taken on an unbelievable size, and even a bit of sophistication, with its fine homes and university, its business blocks and country clubs. It had grown noisily around Sara Atkin; the tide of traffic now banged and clanged on the paved corner that had once been rutty and grass-grown.

But even though a filling station had gone up across the alley on the Seventh Street side, and rather high-priced apartments on the Churchill Avenue side, old Sara would not leave, but stayed on in the fussy house with the walnut hall rack and the marble mantels.

She lived there all alone, too, except for the daily presence of one Jennie Williams, who came ploddingly down Seventh Street each day to work. Once, in Jennie's high school days, Sara had taken her on temporarily until she could find someone else to help. But Jennie had grown fat and 40 waiting for Mrs. Atkin to find another girl.

This morning she came puffingly through the kitchen door in time to see Sara Atkin turning the page of the drugstore calendar on the kitchen wall and pinning back the flapping leaf so that the word "December" stood out boldly.

Old Sara greeted Jennie with a subtle, "Do you know what date this is, Jennie?" She asked the same darkly mysterious question every year, and, as always, Jennie feigned surprise. "Don't tell me it's December a'ready, Mis' Atkin?"

Yes, it was December; old Sara Atkin's own special month—the one for which she lived, the one toward which all the other months led like steps to some shining Taj Mahal. It was the month in which all the children came home.

"It's true, Jennie. Time again to bid the tapers twinkle fair. Did I ever tell you how our family came to use that expression, Jennie?"

Jennie had heard the explanation every year for a quarter of a century, but she obligingly assumed ignorance. "How's that, Mis' Atkin?" As a stooge Jennie Williams could not have been surpassed.

Sara Atkin's white old face took on a glow. "Well, it was years ago. My goodness, I don't know how many—maybe 41 or two; I could figure it out if I took time. But our Dickie was just a little chap—that's Mr. Richard Atkin, you know, my lawyer son—and he was going to speak his first piece in the new schoolhouse on Christmas Eve. The piece he was to give began:

"We hang up garlands everywhere
And bid the tapers twinkle fair."

"When you stop to think about it, Jennie, that's a hard line for anybody to say, let alone a little codger with his first piece. I can just see him—he had on a little brown suit I'd made him and was so round and roly-poly, and he stood up so bravely in front of all of those folks and began so cute:

"'We hang up garlands everywhere
And bid the twapers tinkle tair.'"

"He knew something was wrong—everyone was grinning—and he stopped and tried again, but this time he got it:

"'And bid the taters pinkle tair.'"

"Every one laughed out loud and he said, 'I mean:

"'And tid the bapers finkle fair.'"

Sara Atkin laughed at the little memory so dear to her old heart, and Jennie politely followed suit with as extensive a show of hilarity as one could muster after hearing the anecdote for 25 years.

"Richard never heard the last of it. And after that whenever Christmas was coming we'd always say it was time to bid the tapers twinkle fair. I guess all big families have jokes that way, Jennie."

"I guess yours more than most folks, Mis' Atkin. My, I never knew anybody to make such a hullabaloo over Christmas as you Atkinses do."

It was just faintly possible that a bit of acidity had crept into Jennie's voice. The coming month was not going to be exactly a period of inertia for fat, slow Jennie. But to old Sara it was merely an invitation to indulge in a line of reminiscences, so that it was almost a half hour before Jennie needed to start working.

Jennie Williams was right. The Atkins made much of Christmas festivities.

There are those to whom Christmas means little or nothing; those whose liking for it is more or less superficial; those who worship it with a love that cannot be told. Sara Atkin had always been one of these last. Christmas to her meant the climax of the year, the day for which one lived. It meant vast preparation, the coming together of the clan. She had never been able to understand women to whom it was merely half interesting, sometimes even a cause for complaint. From the first Christmas in the sod house with a makeshift tree for the baby, to the previous year with 21 coming, she had sunk herself in loving preparation for the day. No matter what experiences had preceded it—drought, blizzards, crop failures, financial losses, illness—she had approached The Day with a warmth of gladness, an uplift of the spirit which no other season could bring forth.

In those old pioneer days she had neighbors who possessed no initiative by which to make Christmas gifts out of their meager supplies. She herself had known that it took only love and energy to make them.

There had been two sons and two daughters born to her. They were middle-aged now, but by some strange magic she had transmitted to them this vital love for the Christmas time, so that they, too, held the same intense ardor for the day. In the years that were gone sons and grandsons had wrangled with wives that they must go to Grandma Atkin's for Christmas. As for the daugh-

94

ters and granddaughters, they had made it clear from the times of their engagements that it was not even a subject for debate whether they should attend the family reunion. To the Atkin descendants at large old Sara Atkin *was* Christmas.

So now the annual preparations began. Life took on a rose-colored hue for old Sara, and a dark blue one for Jennie. Rugs came out to be beaten and curtains down to be washed. Permanent beds were made immaculate and temporary ones installed. A dozen cookbooks were consulted and the tree ordered. Jennie in her obesity and obstinacy was urged gently to try to make more effective motions. Once in her happiness old Sara said chucklingly, "Jennie, Doctor Pitkin was wrong. Life begins at 80."

To which Jennie made acrid reply, "Good land, don't tell me you've took up with a new doctor at your age, Mis' Atkin."

Eva, dropping in from a bridge afternoon, found her mother on the couch at the close of a day's preparations, a pan of strung popcorn at her side. The daughter was perturbed, scolded a little. "Mother, what is there about you that makes you attack Christmas this hard way? You'll make yourself sick. Why don't we all go to the University Club? We can get a private room if we get in our bid right away."

"What? A club? On Christmas? Not while I have a roof over my head."

"But you do so many unnecessary things. No one strings popcorn any more for a tree. That was in the days when there weren't so many decorations."

"There's no law against it," said old Sara. "Or is there," she twinkled, "since the government has so much to say?"

In a few days Eva dropped in again. She had something on her mind, was hesitant in getting it out, averted her eyes a bit when she told it. "Mother, I hope I'm not going to disappoint you too much, but Fred and I think our family will have to go to Josephine's for Christmas. She's the farthest away . . . and can't come . . . and would like to have us . . . and . . ." Her voice trailed off apologetically.

Old Sara was sorry. But, "You do what's best," she said cheerily. She must not be selfish. It was not always possible for all of them to be with her, so she would not let it disturb her.

She told Jennie about it next morning. "There will be five less than we thought, Jennie. My daughter, Mrs. Fleming, and Professor Fleming and their daughter's family won't be here."

Jennie was not thrown into a state which one might term brokenhearted, interpreting the guests' attendance as she did in terms of food and dishes.

The next evening Sara Atkin had a long distance call from Arnold. He visited with his mother with alarming lack of toll economy. In fact, it was some little time before he led up to the news that they were not coming. He and Mame and the boys were going to Marian's. Marian's baby was only nine months old, and Marian thought it better for them all to come there.

When she assured him it was all right, old Sara tried her best to keep a quaver out of her voice. In her disappointment she did not sleep well. In the morning she broke the news to Jennie with some slight manipulating

of the truth, inasmuch as she told her there was a faint possibility that not all of Arnold's family might get there.

When the letter from Helen arrived the next day, she had almost a premonition, so that her eyes went immediately down the page to the distressing statement. They were not coming. They couldn't afford it this year, Helen said, not after the drought. It hurt Sara worse than the others. It wasn't a reason. It was an excuse. That wasn't true about not affording it. It had been a bad year of drought, but Carl had his corn loan. If she had died they could have afforded to come to the funeral. And she could not bring herself to tell Jennie that they, too, were not coming. She had too much pride to let Jennie know that Helen and Carl, who had no children to provide for or educate, thought they were too poor to come home for Christmas.

She had scarcely laid the letter and her glasses aside when the phone rang. It was Mr. Schloss telling her that the turkeys were in. "I'll save you two as always, Mis' Atkin?"

"Yes," said old Sara. Two turkeys for no one but herself and Richard and Clarice and their son Jimmie, who was 16. But she would not admit that the Atkin reunion was to be composed of only four people.

Before breakfast the next morning the night letter came in: "Sorry can't come mother stop jimmie has hard cold caught it playing basketball stop hope message doesn't frighten you stop thought let you know right away stop sending packages stop will be thinking of you all day christmas. richard.

Old Sara got up and shut the door between herself and the kitchen, for fear that Jennie would come in and see her before she had gained control of herself. Twenty-one of them. *And not one was coming.* It was unbelievable. She sat stunned, the telegram still in her hand. She tried to reason with herself, but she seemed to have no reasoning powers; tried to comfort herself, but the heart had gone out of her. All her life she had held to a philosophy of helpfulness, but she knew now she was seeing herself as she really was. A great many people who had no relatives for Christmas gatherings made it a point to invite those who were lonely. They went out into the highways and hedges and brought them in. The Bible said to do so. Old Sara didn't want to. Tears filled her old eyes. She didn't want lonely people from the highways and hedges. She wanted her own folks. *She wanted all the Atkins.*

Jennie was at work in the kitchen now. She seemed slower than ever this morning, trudging about heavily in her flat-heeled slippers. Sara did not care, did not hurry her, gave her no extra duties.

The morning half over, the phone rang, and it was Mr. Schloss again. "Ve got de trees dis mornin', Mis' Atkin. Fine nice vons. I tell you first so you can get your choice same as always. Can you come over?"

Jennie was listening, craning her head to hear. Something made old Sara do it. "Yes, I'll come over."

Mr. Schloss led her mysteriously through the store to the back. "I like you to get the pick. Folks all comin', I suppose? I never saw such relations as you got to have dose goot Christmases. Like when I'm a boy in Germany. Most folks now, it ain't so much to dem anymore."

He sent the tree right over by a boy. Sara and Jennie had the big pail ready with the wet gravel in it.

The boy told them Mr. Schloss said he was to stay and put it up. They placed it in the front parlor by the mottled marble fireplace, its slender green tip reaching nearly to the ceiling. Jennie got down the boxes of ornaments and tinsels and placed them invitingly on the mantel. Old Sara started to decorate. She draped and festooned and stood back mechanically to get the effect, her old eyes not seeing anything but her children, her ears not hearing anything but silence louder than ever noise had been.

For the next two days she went on mechanically with preparations. Before Christmas Eve she would rouse herself and ask in some people—the food and decorations must not be wasted. She would probably have Grandma Bremmer and her old maid daughters. They would be glad to get the home cooking, but Christmas had never meant very much to them. It was just another day at the hotel. Not a vital thing. Not a warm, living experience. Not a fundamental necessity, as it was to the Atkins.

In the meantime her pride would not allow her to tell Jennie or the merchants or the occasional caller who dropped in. "Our family reunion is to be cut down quite a bit this year," she would say casually. "Some of them aren't coming."

Some? Not one was coming.

In the late afternoon before Christmas Eve snowflakes began falling, as lazily as though fat Jennie were scattering them. The house was immaculate, everything prepared.

"Shall I put all the table leaves in, Mis' Atkin?" Jennie was asking.

"No," said Old Sara. "You needn't stay to set the table at all. The—the ones that get here will be in time to help."

"I've got a package I'm bringing you in the morning," Jennie informed her.

"So have I one for you, Jennie. Come early . . . we . . . we'll open them by the tree."

"Well, good night then, Mis' Atkin, and Merry Christmas."

"Good night, Jennie—and Merry Christmas."

Jennie was gone and the house was quiet. The snowflakes were falling faster. The house was shining from front to back. Beds were ready. The tree was sparkling with colored lights, packages from all the children under its tinseled branches. The cupboards were filled with good food. So far as preparations were concerned, everything was ready for the family reunion. And no one but herself knew that there was to be no reunion.

Later in the evening she would call up the Bremmers. But in the meantime she would lie down in the back parlor and rest. Strange how very tired she felt, when there had been so little confusion. She pulled a shawl about her and lay down on the old leather couch.

Through the archway she could see the tree, shining in all its bravery, as though trying to be gay and gallant. Then she nodded and it looked far away and small. She dozed, awakened, dozed again. The tiny tree out there now had tufts of cotton from a quilt on it, bits of tinfoil from a package of tea, homemade candles of mutton tallow. It was a queer little cottonwood tree trying to look like a evergreen—a tree such as she had in the pioneer days.

She could not have told the exact moment in which she began to hear them, could not have named the precise time in which she first saw them vaguely through the shadows. But somewhere on the borderland of her consciousness she suddenly realized they were out there under the crude little tree. Arnold was examining a homemade sled, his face alight with boyish eagerness. Eva and Helen were excitedly taking the brown paper wrappings from rag dolls. Dickie was on the floor spinning a top made from empty spools. Every little face was clear, every little figure plain. For a long time she watched them playing under the makeshift tree, a warm glow of happiness suffusing her whole being. Some vague previous hurt she had experienced was healed. Everything was all right. The children were here.

Then she roused, swept her hand over her eyes in the perplexity of her bewilderment, felt herself grow cold and numb with the disappointment of it. The children were not here. When you grew old you must face the fact that you could have them only in dreams.

It was almost dusk outside now, with the falling of the early December twilight. Christmas Eve was descending—the magic hour before the coming of the Child. It was the enchanted time in which all children should seek their homes—the family time. So under the spell of the magic moment was she that when the bell rang and she realized it was not the children, she thought at first that she would not pay any attention to the noisy summons. It would be some kind friend or neighbor whose very kindness would unnerve her. But the habit of years was strong. When one's bell rang, one went to the door.

So she rose, brushed back a straying lock, pulled her wool shawl about her shoulders and went into the hallway, holding her head gallantly.

"Merry Christmas, Mother!" "Merry Christmas, Grandma." It came from countless throats, lustily, joyfully.

"Bid the tapers twinkle fair, Mother."

"He means bid the taters finkle tair, Grandma." Laughter rose noisily.

She could not believe it. Her brain was addled. The vision of the children under the tree had been bright, also. This was another illusion.

But if the figures on the porch were wraiths from some hinterland, they were very substantial ones. If they were apparitions they were then phantoms which wore fur coats and tweeds and knitted sport suits, shadows whose frosty breath came forth in a most unghostly fashion in the cold air of the December twilight.

They were bursting through the doorway now, bringing mingled odors of frost, holly, faint perfumes, food, mistletoe, evergreens; stamping snow from shoes, carrying packages to the chins—Eva and Fred, Arnold and Mame, Dick and Clarice, Helen and Carl, Josephine and her family, Marian with her husband and baby, Richard's Jimmie, and Arnold's boys. They noisily filled the old hall, oozed out into the dining room, backed up the stairway, fell over the tall old walnut hat rack. They did not once cease their loud and merry talking.

"Aren't we the rabble?"

"Did you ever know there were so many Atkins?"

"We look like a movie mob scene."

"The President should give us a silver loving cup or something."

They surged around old Sara Atkin, who had her hand on her throat to stop the tumultuous beating of its pulse.

"But I don't understand. Why did—why did you say you weren't coming?" she was asking feebly of those nearest to her.

Several feminine voices answered simultaneously— Eva and Helen and Dick's wife. "To save you working your fingers to the bone, Mother. The way you always slave—it's just ridiculous."

"We decided that the only way to keep you from it was just to say we weren't any of us coming, and then walk in the last minute and bring all the things."

"Carl and I couldn't think of an excuse." It was Helen. "So we laid it to the poor old drought. And we'd a perfectly dreadful time—writing and phoning around to get it planned, what every one should do. I brought the turkey all ready for the oven—Carl, where's the turkey? Get it from the car."

"Fred and I have the tree outside and—" Eva broke off to say, "Why, Mother, you've a tree?"

Clarice said, "Oh, look, folks, her packages are under it. And she thought she was going to open them all by herself. Why that makes me feel teary."

Old Sara Atkin sat down heavily in a hall chair. There were 21 of them—some of them flesh of her flesh. They had done this for her own good, they thought. Twenty-one of them—and not one had understood how much less painful it is to be tired in your body than to be weary in your mind, how much less distressing it is to have an ache in your bones than to have a hurt in your heart.

There was the oyster supper, gay and noisy. There were stockings hung up and additional Christmas wreaths. There was Christmas music from a radio and from a phonograph and from the more-or-less nonmusical throats of a dozen Atkins. There were Chrismas stories and Christmas jokes. There were wide-eyed children put to bed and a session of grown people around the tree. There were early lights on Christmas morning and a great crowd of Atkins piling out in the cold of their bedrooms and calling raucous Merry Christmases to one another. There was a hasty unwanted breakfast with many pert remarks about hurrying up. There was the great family circle about the fireplace and the tree with Arnold Atkin, Jr., calling out the names on the gifts, accompanied by a run of family flippancies. There were snowbanks of tissue paper and entanglements of string. There was the turkey dinner. And through it all, after the manner of the Atkin clan, there was constant talk and laughter.

The noise beat against the contented mind of Sara Atkin all day, like the wash of breakers against the sturdy shore.

All of this transpired until the late Christmas afternoon, when the entire crowd went up to Eva's new home near the campus.

"Don't you feel like coming too, Mother?"

"No, I'm a little tired and I'll just rest awhile before you come back."

They were gone. The house was appallingly quiet after the din of the passing day. There was no sound but the pad-padding of Jennie Williams in the kitchen.

Old Sara lay down on the couch in the back parlor. Through the archway she could see a portion of the disheveled front room, over which a cyclone apparently had swept. The tree with its lights still shining gaily stood in the midst of the debris.

In her bodily weariness she nodded, dozed, awakened, dozed. Suddenly the tree blurred, then grew enormous; the green of its branches became other trees, a vast number of them springing from the shadows. They massed together in a huge cedar forest, some candle laden and some electric lighted, but all gallant with Christmas cheer. Under the branches were countless children and grown people. And then suddenly she almost laughed aloud, to see that they were all her own. There were a dozen Arnolds, a dozen Helens—all her boys and girls at all their ages playing under all the trees which had ever been trimmed for them. It was as though in one short moment she had seen together the entire Christmases of the 60 years.

She roused and smiled at the memory of having seen such a wondrous sight. *Well, I suppose there'll not be many more for me*, she thought, *but I've passed on the tapers. They all love it as I do. They won't forget to light the tapers after—after I'm gone.*

Then she sat up and threw off her shawl with vehement gesture. "Fiddlesticks! Imagine me talking that way about dying—as if I were an old woman. I'm only 81. I'm good for a dozen more Christmases. My body isn't feeble—at least, only at times. As for my mind, my mind's just as clear as a bell."

She rose and went out to the dining room. Jennie Williams was trudging about putting away the last of the best dishes. Some of the women had helped her, but there were a dozen things she had been obliged to finish herself. She was tired and cross with the unnecessary work and the undue commotion. Her feet hurt her. She liked the peaceful, slow days better.

"Well, Jennie, it's all over," old Sara said happily. "We had a good time, same as always. We've had a grand day to bid the tapers twinkle fair. Jennie, did I ever tell you how we Atkins happened to start using that expression?"

Jennie jerked her heavy body about and opened her mouth to answer determinedly, for she felt her provocation was great. But she stopped suddenly at the sight of old Sara Atkin standing in the doorway. For old Sara's sweet white face glowed with an inner light, and the illumination from the tree behind her gave the appearance of a halo around her head. Suddenly Jennie Williams had a strange thought about old Sara. It was that Mary the Mother might have looked that way when she was old.

"No," said Jennie kindly. "I don't believe you ever have told me, Mis' Atkin. How *did* you?"

Why Carolyn Didn't Go to the Christmas Party

Arthur Milward

Some Christmas stories pose more questions than they answer. This is one of them. What can we do when God says no? When there is a child with a whole lifetime ahead— then, suddenly, it is all over. What then? What answers can possibly make sense?

Arthur Milward, living in Kennett Square, Pennsylvania, a professional free-lance writer, remembers days etched in such pain that they seared the membranes of his heart, remembers his own son, dying there in that London hospital. And remembers, like yesterday, Carolyn.

She wouldn't smile at me today, Daddy," Adrian confided, a worried look in his gray eyes. "She seemed sad." And with a perception beyond his four years, "Maybe she's afraid she's not going to get better—not ever."

I glanced across the hospital ward toward Carolyn's bed. When I arrived to visit my small son, she would frequently come across to Ady's bed and join us and sit and chat for a while.

But not today. She was lying, fully dressed, on her bed, curled up into a ball, with her back toward the other occupants of the ward. Clearly, right now Carolyn didn't feel like talking to anyone. I decided to leave well enough alone.

"You're probably right," I assured Adrian. "She's most likely not feeling good today. Maybe she'll be feeling better tomorrow." And I left it at that because another problem that demanded my attention had come up. This problem, too, concerned Carolyn.

I had been visiting the terminal ward at the Hospital for Sick Children in London to see my little boy so regularly and for so long that I had come to feel like, and to be treated almost as, a member of the staff. So when it came time to plan for the ward Christmas party and the problem came up, the Sister and staff nurse in charge of the ward sought my opinion.

They were aware that I was a Christian, and they knew I had been a missionary, so I suppose they felt that I was therefore somehow qualified to provide a ruling on what was, in effect, sort of a theological question.

The problem concerned Carolyn and the forthcoming Christmas party. Carolyn, you see, was Jewish. Her parents were Orthodox, and she never accompanied the other children to the hospital chapel on Sunday evenings for the church service.

Would it be proper, queried Sister Palmer, for Carolyn to attend the Christmas party? It was, after all, a Christian celebration. Did I think her parents would object? And if she didn't attend, what should be done with her while the party was in progress?

The nurses were not wholly satisfied with my comments. It would not, I pointed out, be a religious-type party. And, to my mind, a much more important question was whether Carolyn herself wanted to be there or not.

The nurses were not fully convinced I had the solution, so for the time being the question was left open. I returned to the ward to help my little son get ready for bed before I had to leave for home 40 miles away.

Several days passed. Each day as I visited the hospital and talked with my little boy I saw Carolyn. She seemed about the same as usual, a bit depressed perhaps, but that was to be expected.

Carolyn was the oldest of eight children currently in the terminal ward. None of them could reasonably anticipate much of a future, but most of the boys and girls were too young to realize their situation fully.

Carolyn, however, was 10 years old, going on 11, and she had a pretty good idea of what was in store for her. A victim of a leukemic-type disease, she had overheard enough to realize that her prospects were, to put it conservatively, not bright.

Three or four days after Adrian's initial observation of her evident depression, Carolyn joined us early in the evening as I was putting Ady to bed before leaving to catch my train. I noted the dark shadows under her eyes. She looked desperately tired.

I knew little of the progress of her disease. Only what I had overheard from the conversation of the doctors and nurses. The chart at the foot of each child's bed was an identification chart only. All the data it bore

was the name, age, sex, and religion (if any) of the child, together with the name of the doctor in charge. All the pertinent information concerning the diagnosis, progress of his or her condition, and prognosis was filed away from prying eyes in Sister's office.

Carolyn pulled my head down to her level where she sat on the edge of Adrian's bed and spoke into my ear as Ady was just dropping off to sleep. "Can you stay and talk to me a little while when Ady's asleep?" she requested. "Will you, *please?*"

I was on the point of telling her that I really had to leave to catch my train home. Something in her face, however, stopped me. She had a look of despair in her big, dark eyes, a desperate look I found almost terrifying in one so young.

"All right," I agreed. "As soon as Ady's really sleeping. Give me a minute to call home and I'll be with you."

I went to the nurses' sitting room and phoned home. I assured my wife that Ady was all right, that there was no change. Then I told her something had come up and I would have to get a later train than usual. She was not to worry. I would explain when I got home.

I returned to the ward where Carolyn awaited me. She looked relieved, almost as if she had feared I would not return.

"Thank you," she said. "I've got to talk to somebody or I'll burst. Daddy's away again in Switzerland on a business trip, and Mommy always bursts into tears if I say anything except 'I feel fine.'"

I nodded. I had met Carolyn's parents briefly when their visits to the hospital coincided with mine. Her father, a tall, distinguished-looking man, was one of those parents who was totally unable to accept what was happening to his only daughter. He evidently, I gathered, felt that by denying the unthinkable, he would make it go away. He was frequently away in Europe on business. Her mother was an affectionate, emotional sort of person. They both obviously adored their daughter.

I secured a wheelchair and wheeled Carolyn into the now empty playroom adjoining the ward. Toys were still strewn around the floor from the afternoon's activities. I swept a couple of plush rabbits and a teddy bear from a leather-covered armchair, carefully lifted Carolyn in my arms and settled her into the armchair. I drew up another chair and sat down close to her.

For a minute or two neither of us spoke. I can never forget what I saw: a slender figure in a blue, lace-trimmed robe and, incongruously, pink slippers. She looked lost, almost, in the big armchair, and terribly, unbearably vulnerable. Her dark, luminous eyes were fixed earnestly on mine. Two big tears escaped and rolled slowly down her cheeks.

I leaned forward involuntarily and took both her hands in my own. I didn't know quite what to say. "Well, Carolyn," I began inanely, "it won't be long now till Christmas."

She looked at me almost uncomprehendingly. "I don't care about Christmas," she assured me, almost fiercely. "Christmas is for Christians, anyway."

I realized suddenly that I had nothing to say that Carolyn wanted to hear. She needed, desperately needed, a listener.

The words came slowly at first, haltingly, as if she were dragging them up from who knows what unknown depths. She held onto my hands and soon the words began to pour out, faster and faster. A deluge, a torrent, of words.

She told me of her "Christmas"—of the celebration of the eight days of Hanukkah. Her eyes shone as she told me of her grandmother lighting the menorah, the eight-branched candelabrum, of the songs and prayers that accompanied the Jewish celebration. She released my hands and gesticulated as she recounted the ancient story of the liberation of the Jewish people by the heroic Maccabeans.

I listened, mesmerized almost, and my thoughts turned to dogs, and Phoenician women, and crumbs.

Suddenly, her mood changed. Exhausted, she sank back in her chair and her voice became almost a whisper. "I know," she said, her voice breaking. "I know I'm going to die."

Her tears fell freely now. "You know," she said between sobs, "I can't believe it, but I know it's true. . . . You know," she said again, "I want to have a boyfriend. I want a boy to tell me he loves me and can't live without me. I want to grow up and get married. I want to have children of my own. I want to live." Her voice broke.

She threw her long, dark hair back from her face and looked straight at me, her small fists clenched, willing me to do something about it.

She gave a despairing yelp—I don't know what else to call it—like a small animal caught in a trap, and then threw herself into my arms. "I don't want to die!" she wailed.

What does one say to a 10-year-old girl who doesn't want to die?

I held her close to me and stroked her shining dark hair. I told her she was beautiful. I wept along with her and felt totally inadequate.

She didn't say any more. She just clung to me, sobbing, for a long time. After a while she quieted down and finally fell asleep with her head on my shoulder. I called for a nurse, and together we carried her back to the ward and put her in her bed. I tried to compose myself and washed my face in cold water before I left for the railroad depot and my train home. It was late by this time. Adrian was still fast asleep.

When I visited my little son the following afternoon I saw immediately that the bed across from Ady's—Carolyn's bed—was occupied by a little boy. He was about 7 years old. He told me his name was Jimmy.

I asked no questions and nobody made any comment. It wasn't that sort of ward. Nobody, not even the youngest, ever asked why a bed was suddenly empty or occupied by a newcomer. Everybody, even the youngest, sensed it was something that nobody could bear to talk about.

Later, however, Sister Palmer drew me to one side and told me that Carolyn had lived only halfway through the night.

"Her mother and grandmother were there," she told me in answer to my question. "Her father was in Geneva on business. We phoned, but of course he didn't arrive in time."

I saw Carolyn's parents once more just a couple days later as I was arriving to visit my son. They were just leaving. They had been up to the ward to collect what lawyers refer to as "the effects." Her father, who looked stunned, carried a small blue suitcase. Her mother, weeping, looked for all the world like a small child who had just been scolded. She dangled a flaxen-haired doll by one leg.

I bowed slightly as they approached. The mother put out a hand as if to detain me.

The father set down the suitcase and took both my hands. "You're Ady's father," he said in his heavily accented English. "Carolyn spoke of you. Thank you." His eyes filled with tears.

I bowed again. There was nothing to say.

So Carolyn missed the Christmas party after all. Most of the parents were there, and everyone studiously worked at having a good time. To be fair, the little ones did have fun, I am sure.

There was a tree, and Santa Claus, carols, games, lots of ice cream and cookies, and records playing "Rudolph the Red-nosed Reindeer." There really wasn't much mention of Jesus or religion at all.

I wondered what Carolyn would have thought of it.

Pandora's Books

Joseph Leininger Wheeler

It was just another bookstore—well, another used-book store. And what could possibly happen in a bookstore that would be worth remembering?

PROLOGUE

It would be remembered as "the year with no spring." All the more surprising because it had been a bitterly cold winter, complete with record snowfall, frequent ice-storms, traffic gridlock on the beltway around Washington, D.C., closed airports, and snow days—longed-for by children and teachers alike.

At first, people assumed it to be a fluke. Although the iced over Potomac and Severn Rivers were only now beginning to break up, the honking geese were flying north already, attuned to their planet's moods in ways humans will never understand.

And the cherry blossoms down on the Tidal Basin, and the daffodils . . . they couldn't possibly be blooming this early! But they were. And those who delayed but a day missed Jefferson's lagoon at its loveliest, for unseasonably warm air, coupled with sudden wind, stripped the blossoms from the unbelieving trees.

Usually, the multi-hued azalea and the dogwood of pink and white ravish the senses for weeks every spring.

Not so this year; they came and went in a matter of days. By early April the thermometer had already climbed to 100, and now schools began to close because of the heat, instead of the cold.

Once entrenched, the heat dug in and the mercury kept climbing. Even the spring rains failed to come, and farmers shook their heads, trembling in their mortgages. Plants dried up, lawns turned brown, and centuries-old trees dropped their already yellowish leaves in abject defeat.

Tourists stayed home, making sizzling Washington a veritable ghost town. For the first time in recent memory, one could park anywhere one went—no waiting, no endless circling.

And for those Washingtonians who did not have air-conditioning in home, office, and cars it was hell. One couldn't even escape by boat, for prolonged calms plagued the Chesapeake, interspersed by blasting gales of fierce, tinder-dry winds.

On TV weather maps the entire eastern seaboard turned brown in early April and stayed brown, altering only to a deeper hue of brown. There developed a sort of morbid fascination in watching as heat record after heat record fell before that immovable weather front.

When the weather reporters trumpeted the glad news that come Memorial Day weekend the siege would be lifted and blessed coolness from Canada would flow in, most people greeted it as a second Armistice Day, a time to climb out of their bunkers and celebrate.

Traffic jams clogged roads everywhere, and Highway 50 became a parking lot from Washington to Ocean City. The euphoria ran so high people didn't seem to mind. They got out of their vehicles, set up their lawn chairs on the median, threw frisbees back and forth, and ate picnic lunches. One enterprising caravan of college students even found enough room between their cars to play a screwy sort of volleyball in the middle of the Chesapeake Bay Bridge.

But some people find happiness in places other than the beach. Places like bookstores. Used-book stores . . . Pandora's bookstore.

* * *

Oh, it feels so great to have a cool day again! mused Jennifer as she drove out onto Highway 50 with the top down for the first time in, well, it *seemed* a year. It felt good to let her hair fly loose in the wind. As Annapolis loomed ahead, she veered off on Riva Road, then headed south on Highway 2. Stick-um'd to her checkbook were Amy's directions.

"Oh, Jen, you'll just *love* it!" her closest friend had raved. "It's unlike any other bookstore you have ever seen."

Jennifer, a veteran of hundreds of used-book stores, strongly doubted that, but not wanting to flatly contradict her friend she merely mumbled a muffled, "Oh?"

Amy, noting the doubt written on her face (Jennifer never *had* been able to keep a secret for her expressive face gave it away every time) merely grinned and looked wise. "Just you wyte, 'enry 'iggens; just you wyte!" she caroled.

In the months following that challenge, several other friends had rhapsodized about this one-of-a-kind bookstore, each report torquing up her curiosity another notch. Now, on this absolutely perfect late May day, she saw no reason to delay further: she would see this hyped-way-beyond-its-worth place for herself. After all, there were no other claims on her day.

More's the pity, she told herself. And her truant memory wafted her backward, without ever asking permission, to a time when she *had* been needed, *had* been wanted, *had* been loved. *Or,* she qualified to herself, *at least I thought he loved me!*

It had been one of those childhood romances adults so often chuckle about. The proverbial boy next door. They had played together all those preschool years, inside one of their homes in bad weather; outside the rest of the time. When school started, they entered first grade together.

He carried her books, fought anyone who mistreated her, and at home they studied together. He had been the first boy to hold her hand, the first she had kissed. Their parents had merely laughed in that condescending way adults have about young love and prophesied, "Puppy love *never* lasts. Just watch; they'll each find someone else."

But they didn't find "somebody else." Not even when puberty messed them up inside, recontoured their bodies, redirected their thoughts. Each remained the other's all.

They even chose the same college and continued studying together. They went to concerts and art galleries together, hiked the mountains together, walked the beaches barefoot together, haunted bookstores together, went to parties together, and even attended church together.

So it had come as no surprise that spring break of their senior year when, walking among the dunes near Cape Hatteras, he asked her to marry him. And there was no hesitation in her delighted "Yes, Bill!"

That it somehow lacked passion, that there was little yearning for the other physically, didn't seem to matter. Hadn't their relationship stood the test of time? How much longer than 20 years would it take to *know*, for goodness' sake!

So the date had been set, the wedding party chosen, the bridal gown and attendants' dresses made, the flowers ordered, the tuxes measured, the minister and chapel secured, the honeymoon destination booked, the apartment they would live in arranged for, the wedding invitations sent out.

And then, 36 hours before the wedding, her world had caved in on her. He had come over and asked if they could talk.

"Of course!" she had smiled, chalking up the tense look on his face to groom jitters.

They sat down in their favorite swing on the back porch and looked out at the yard, already festive for the reception to be held there. Her smile faded quickly as she took in his haggard face, his eyes with dark circles around them. Premonition froze her into glacial immobility. Surely it couldn't be what deep down she sensed it would be. Not after all these years!

But it was. He could only stammer brokenly the chopped up words and phrases that would amputate two dreams that had grown within hours of becoming one.

He had found someone whose presence—or absence—raised him to the skies or plunged him to the depths; someone who ignited his hormones to such an extent that life without her was unthinkable. Bill hadn't gone far before his face turned scarlet and he began to sputter.

In mercy, Jennifer broke in. "Don't say anything more, Bill," she cried in a strangely ragged voice. "You can't force love—not the real lifetime kind. I—I'd far rather know this now than later." She paused for control.

Bill could only sit there miserably, his head in his hands.

So it was up to her to finish this thing. She knew she would always love him; he had been her best friend for almost as far back as she could remember. And there is no trapdoor to open and dump such things through. The memories remain *always* and cannot be so easily disposed of.

He couldn't bring himself to face her parents, so after a few more minutes they stood up, there was one last hug—and he walked away.

She salvaged a bit of her battered pride by calling off the wedding herself. That was the hardest thing she had ever done. Numbly, she phoned them all, but gave no reasons. They would know why soon enough, if they didn't already. And so her marital dreams had died.

A year passed. Then another, and another, until six years separated her from that fateful parting, separated the girl from the woman. On one side, trust and unconditional acceptance; on the other, suspicion and reserve.

During that first two years she turned down all the men who asked her out. But gradually, as her blud-

geoned self-esteem began to get up off the floor, she belatedly realized that life must go on, that she must not wall herself off from living. So she began to date again, but not very often. Nine months of the year the children in her third-grade classroom were her world. During the other three she took graduate work, traveled, wrote, visited art galleries, attended plays, concerts, and operas. Often alone, but sometimes with Amy or her brother James.

She sometimes wondered if she would ever find the kind of mate Bill had found, the kind of magnetism that would call her even across the proverbial "crowded room." Would there ever be someone who would set her heart singing? Who would be the friend Bill had been, but who would also arouse a passionate yearning to be his physical, mental, social, and spiritual mate? And once in a while she would wonder, *Why is it so difficult to find the one? Is there something wrong with me?*

So the long years passed. She completed her masters at Johns Hopkins, and she was invariably doing *something,* anything, to avoid admitting to herself that she was unutterably lonely. None of her diversions worked. Not one.

* * *

Oh, she had almost missed her road! She slammed on the brakes, almost getting rear-ended in the process, and turned left. Three and seven-tenths miles, Amy had said. Sure enough, there loomed the sign: "PANDORA'S BOOKS."

Gotta be a story here somewhere, she smiled. Now she slowed and turned into an ancient-looking brick gate-way. Just inside, another sign announced that this was a wildlife sanctuary. *Some bookstore!* The road snaked its way through first-growth trees (one of the only such stands of timber left on this part of the Chesapeake, according to a sign). Here and there azalea, rhododendron, and wild laurel bushes banked the road.

She slowed the Camaro to a crawl to give some deer time to get off the road. Birds seemed to be everywhere—cardinals, goldfinch, sparrows, even a couple of bluebirds—and high overhead, hawks and gulls. It seemed incongruous, this close to the Washington metroplex of 6 million people, to discover such solitude.

At last the road straightened out and dropped down into the strangest parking lot she had ever seen. Following directions from a sign, she drove into another grove of trees until she came to a pull-in unoccupied by a car or van. After putting the top up and locking the car, she found a path to the beach. She sensed the water's edge before she could see it, and now she could plainly hear the *ca-ca-ca-ca* of the gulls. Suddenly, there it was: blinding white clapboard, framed by the silver-flecked blue of the Chesapeake. No clouds overhead today, only seagulls; and on the water, like swans taking flight, sailboats, as far as the eye could see. She stopped, transfixed, and inwardly spoke to her best Friend.

Lord, thank You for this day, this almost-too-beautiful-to-be-true day.

She had always been more intense than any of her friends, more deeply affected by beauty.

Before going in she added a rather strange postscript. *Lord, please let only good things happen to me today.* Then she opened the door and walked in.

Classical music played softly, meshing wondrously with the lapping of the waves on the shore, the cry of the gulls, and the occasional raucous croak that could come only from the long throat of a great blue heron.

And ah, that one-of-a-kind fragrance of old books, which to booklovers is the true wine of life! This place was blessedly different. She set out to analyze it and find out why.

First of all, it was clean, she decided. Not antiseptically so—just close enough. No grime besmirched the shelves, books, walls, windows, or the floor. Second, although the store contained tens of thousands of books, there was no perception of clutter or of being engulfed by the sheer mass of it all. Why that was so was easy to see: masses of books were broken up by old prints, paintings, sculpture, bric-a-brac, and flowers. *Real* flowers. She could tell that by their fragrance. And the windows . . . *open* windows, to let in the outside world. Or just enough of it. And there were benches and soft chairs everywhere, graced by lamps of great beauty.

Quickly, she discovered that the art work tied in perfectly with the genre displayed on the shelves. For instance, Remingtons and Russells dominated the walls of the Western room, supplemented by dust jacket originals, magazine art, movie posters, lobby cards, and old photographs. The adolescent/youth section had as its focal center a wondrous display of Maxfield Parrish, with its pièce de résistance being the largest print she'd ever seen of his *Ecstasy*. Blowups of dust jackets, paperbacks, and magazine art graced the walls in just the right places.

And amazingly, different music played softly in every room. In the Western room could be heard most of the old standard Western artists, from The Sons of the Pioneers to Eddy Arnold. In the religion and philosophy room she heard the great music of the church. Lilting, happy music children love flowed from the children's room.

But best of all was the literature and general fiction room. For one thing, it dominated the seaward side of the second story. And on walls where no direct sunlight would fade what hung there, she saw faithfully reproduced copies of old masters: Zurburan, Titian, Leonardo, Ribera, Caravaggio, DelaTour, and Rembrandt. A massive stone fireplace anchored the southeastern corner. Just to its right stood a nine-foot grand piano. On its shiny surface was flopped in abandoned comfort as beautiful a Himalayan as Jennifer had ever seen. Without even thinking, she crossed the room and reached out her hand, allowing it to be sniffed before she ventured to scratch the cat's head and massage its ears. A loud purring told her that she had been accepted into the narrow circle that could induce purring.

Jennifer crossed to one of the open windows, leaned against the sill, and gazed across the silver-flecked blue water. Then, ever so softly, floating out of the very walls it seemed, she heard those haunting first bars of Chopin's *Étude in E*. It was just too much; her intensely passionate nature could handle only so much circuit overload. She lost all track of time or reality.

* * *

Coming up the stairs with a load of books for restocking, Arthur sighed. On this seemingly perfect day he longed to be outside. But so did his employees, so he had let most of them go. Reluctantly. As he heard *Étude in E*, he slowed his pace. No matter how often he heard it, that *Étude* got him every time. Something in its melody brought an ache, reminded him that he was alone, incomplete. Thus his normal defenses melted like wax when he stepped into the room that housed his classics—and stopped, rooted to the floor, when he saw the figure staring out the window. Her sapphire blue dress draped long, loose, and Maxfield Parrish classical; her complexion cameo ivory; her long hair a copperish flame; her ankles and Teva-sandled feet slim and graceful. A pre-Raphaelite painting suddenly come to life there in the room. He dared not breathe lest he break her trance.

Subconsciously, he weighed the external pieces that added up to the totality. *No*, he concluded, *she is not beautiful, though she has classical features and classical form. But she's alive, as alive as any woman I have ever seen.* He watched as the music internalized in her heart and soul and overflowed into her face [that face that always mirrored her inner self, in spite of all efforts to control it]. A tear glistened in her eye, the color of which he could not from that angle see, and slowly made a pathway down her cheek. But in her trance she did not even notice it. Strange, even though he'd never seen her before, he yearned to wipe that tear away and find out what caused it . . . if it was the *Étude*, or if it was something more.

* * *

Something woke her, told her she was no longer

CIMH6-8

alone. She turned slightly and saw him standing there, photographing her with his blue-gray eyes. (Hers, he now discovered, were an amazing emerald green.) Gradually, as the mists of her trance dissipated, he came into full focus. He stood 6'2", dark-brown hair salted with premature gray; trim, physically fit. Dressed well, in a button-up chambray shirt, khaki dockers, and slip-on loafers. In his mid-to-late 30s, she guessed.

But his face . . . she felt instinctively that this man standing there knew pain, for it etched his face. Especially did she note it in the ever-so-slight droop of a mouth that seemed made for smiling. His eyes, she concluded, were wonderfully kind, filled with tenderness and concern, and for such ammunition she had no defense. Until that moment, she had never needed any.

Feeling a familiar softness rubbing against his leg, he looked down and smiled. She liked that smile and wished to prolong its stay. Clearing her throat, she spoke just one word, "Yours?"

And his smile grew broader as he tenderly picked up the purring cat, cradled it in his muscular arms, and announced, "Pandora."

She laughed, a delightfully throaty laugh, and retorted, "So here is the *real* owner of all these books!"

He laughed too. "Yes, well, it's a long story. If you're not in a hurry, I'll tell you."

I'm not in a hurry, she decided. *Never have I been in less of one in all my life.*

So they sat down on opposite ends of a sofa, and he told her the saga of a Himalayan kitten who got into *everything* (hence, her name), and how she had wrapped her tiny little soul around his when things weren't going

very well for him. (Jennifer sensed that admittance to be a major understatement.) So when certain developments made possible this bookstore, in gratitude, he had named it in the cat's honor.

And he smiled again. "It *is* her bookstore. . . . I'm sure she feels it is hers, perhaps more so than a human ever could. And our customers, well, the people who come here feel she is boss. Everyone asks about her, and no one ever wants to leave without paying his or her respects." He chuckled again. "I'm not so important; not many feel short-changed if they leave without seeing me."

I'm afraid—I'm very afraid . . . that I would, she thought, but did not say so.

So interested did she become in the story of this wonderfully different bookstore that she kept at him until the entire story spilled out. Even—or, perhaps, *especially*—a brief account of the motivation for it: the failure of a relationship central in his life. He did not elaborate.

Other booklovers came and went, eyed the man, woman, and dozing cat on the couch, attempted to listen in, then reluctantly moved on. Three times they suffered interruptions: once for a customer downstairs, once for a phone call, and once by refreshments brought up by the assistant manager. Noticing Jennifer's raised eyebrows, he explained that fresh-brewed coffee (straight and decaf) and herbal tea were always ready on both floors, as were bagels and cookies, cold sodas, and bottles of fruit juice.

"Yeah," he admitted, "coffee's one of my besetting sins . . . the jumpstart that gets me going. Maybe it isn't very smart to mix coffee and snacks with books, but real booklovers rarely mistreat books. No one's wrecked a book yet because of it. There's no smoking, though! I can't stand it, and"—he looked down at the sleeping cat on his lap—"neither can Pandora."

Suddenly Jennifer looked at her watch and jumped to her feet. "I can't believe it! Where has the day gone? So sorry, but I gotta run. Thanks so much for everything, but I'm late for an appointment. But I'll be back! Bye-bye, Pandora." She stooped to give the cat one last scratch under the chin, then she was gone, without so much as revealing her name. *But then,* Arthur mused, *neither did I!*

Although there was not a cloud in the sky, a partial eclipse darkened the sun with her departure. For Arthur, the day had lost its brightness. The droop came back to his lip, but not—not quite so pronounced as before.

* * *

Jennifer stayed away for nearly two weeks, even though each day she felt the magnetic pull. She recoiled from her inner yearning to return. *How silly!* she scolded herself. *How ridiculous to blow out of proportion a simple little conversation. He'd probably talk like that to anyone who came by and asked the same questions. After all, he's in the business to make customers and sell books!*

Finally, thoroughly confused by her inner turbulence, she went back—and he wasn't there. But books are books, and she soon lost herself among them. She wanted to ask about him but could find no reason that didn't seem transparently obvious. However, she did find the books in the vicinity of the check-out stands to be unusually interesting. She kept taking them off the shelves, one at a time, studying them intently, then re-turning them to the shelves, all without remembering anything about them! She blushed crimson when it suddenly came to her what she was doing. *You foolish, foolish schoolgirl!* Sheepishly, she put the last book back on the shelf and moved toward the next room.

She had not waited in vain, however. While she was passing the first cash register, she heard someone ask the clerk where the boss was. She slowed her pace.

"Mr. Bond?" the clerk responded.

"Yes, of course! Mr. Bond!"

"Oh, uh, he didn't tell me where he was going."

Jennifer's sharp ears then picked up a whispered jab from the clerk at the next register. "But you surely wish he had, huh?"

Jennifer sneaked a look. The face of the first speaker flamed scarlet, her blush speaking volumes. *So that's the way the wind blows,* she thought. She appraised the girl carefully: young (at most, mid-20s); statuesque, with midnight-black hair (undoubtedly Spanish). Strikingly beautiful . . .

Even more confused than when she came in, Jennifer hurried out of the bookstore without even looking up Pandora. She was disturbed, angry, and more than a little jealous of this girl who got to work there all the time.

* * *

The three-digit heat returned after the Memorial Day reprieve, and the steamy humidity slowed life to a gasping crawl. Since it was patently too hot to do other than wilt like an unwatered impatien, Jennifer returned again to Pandora's Books.

Looking for him—but not looking for him—she reconnoitered her way through the various rooms, restless as a child the last afternoon of school. Then she saw him sitting on an easy chair by the fireplace, a portable phone at his ear. And curled around the back of his neck like a fur stole (and just as limp) was Pandora.

Her eyes twinkling, she surreptitiously edged her way out of the room, assuming he had not seen her. Eventually, she gravitated back to the children's room, in the center of which was a sunken playground. Apparently, there were *always* children playing there. After browsing a while, she found Alcott's *Flower Fables*, a book she had always wanted to read but had never been able to find. Sinking into a soft chair with a seraphic sigh of pure joy, she opened its covers.

But she was not to sink into another world so easily. Across from her a sandy-haired boy of about 5 was vainly trying to capture his mother's attention. "Mama, Mama, please, Mama, will you—"

"Oh, don't bother me!" the woman snapped.

Undeterred, the little boy persisted. "But Mama, I found this pretty book, and, uh, I wonder if you'd—"

"Oh, for pity's sake, will you leave me alone?" she snarled.

The boy recoiled as if struck and, lips quivering, backed away, casting one last look at the unyielding face of his mother, engrossed in an Agatha Christie thriller. He turned and headed toward a dark-haired woman who was restocking books across the room. His courage wavered as he approached the clerk.

By now Jennifer had forgotten her book completely. *How will the Spanish beauty respond to a child's need?* she asked herself. She didn't have to wait long to find out for the woman, on being tapped on the leg by little fingers, whirled around in surprise, but she did not smile. She had been enduring a raging migraine that afternoon. Milliseconds later her dark eyes scanned the room to see if anyone had seen. Satisfied that no one had [Jennifer was watching her through veiled eyes, a trick women have that men do not], she brusquely turned her back to the child, and continued restocking the shelf.

The little boy didn't cry. He didn't say anything at all. He merely turned around and just stood there, the book still in his hand, lips trembling, and a tear finding its way down his cheek.

It was just too much! Mother or no mother, clerk or no clerk, Jennifer swiftly left her seat and swooped down like a protective hen. Kneeling down, she spoke words kind and gentle as she tenderly wiped away his tears. "Can *I* help, dear?"

But he had been hurt that afternoon, hurt terribly, and was no longer as trusting as he had been only minutes before. He just looked at her, eyes still puddling. She, respecting his space and his selfhood, didn't touch him again—only waited with tenderness in her eyes. It was no contest. An instant later, vanquished by those soft eyes, he was in her arms, his eyes wet, his little shoulders heaving, but making not a sound.

Across the room, his mother continued reading.

When the little body had stopped shaking and the tears had ceased to flow, Jennifer led him to a nearby couch, sat down, and drew him to her. Then she asked him about the book. As he slowly turned the pages and read some of the words, she helped him with the others and explained the illustrations. A look of joy transfigured his face, and excited comprehension filled his voice . . . if one had been there to see it.

Arthur, who had entered the room just in time to catch the entire tableau—*had* seen it. But Jennifer did not see *him*, neither then nor when she took the boy across the room to find another book, his hand held trustingly in hers.

Withdrawing quietly from the scene, Arthur returned to his office, asked his secretary to field all his calls and inquiries, and shut the door. He walked over to the window and looked unseeingly out on the iron-gray bay.

* * *

The next time, she came on a rainy afternoon. Evidently a lot of other people agreed with her that a bookstore was the best place to be on such a day. Long lines piled up behind the cash registers, and many people waited with questions. The clerks, she noticed, tried to be helpful and answered all questions politely and with the obvious willingness to go the second mile. They knew many customers by name.

Even the Spanish girl. From time to time, Jennifer saw the girl turn to see if a certain gentleman remained in his office. When Mr. Bond finally did come out, the girl's cheeks flamed as she looked everywhere but in his direction. A number of people clustered around him, asking questions, each one receiving that same warm smile and attitude of eager helpfulness.

Then the Spanish girl went up to her boss to ask a question. Jennifer didn't fail to notice both the smile he gave his lovely clerk and the rapt expression in the girl's eyes.

She moved on to the American writers section, looking for some of her favorite authors. *Oh, what a selection of Harold Bell Wright! I've never seen this many in one place before!* She took down a dust-jacketed *Exit*. No sooner had she done so than she felt a presence behind her.

"Are you into Wright?" a familiar voice asked.

She turned, smiled—(*I like her dimples*, Arthur observed)—and said, "Well, sort of. I've read five or six, but I've never seen this one . . . or, for that matter, a number of the others here. Rarely do I see more than a few of his books in any one place."

"Well, there's a reason for that, uh, Miss—it *is* Miss?"

"Yes." She found his steady gaze, kindly though it was, more than a bit disconcerting. "My last name is O'Riley."

"Mine," he grinned a little wickedly, "is Bond. But not James." He had obviously used this line many times before. "Arthur Bond."

"And I answer to Jennifer," she said, blushing.

He returned the conversation to the book she held.

"Well, Miss O'Riley, Wright books are hard to get and harder to keep in stock. May I ask which ones you've read?"

"Well, the first of his books I read when I was only 17. Read it one beautiful day in California's Feather River Canyon. I was visiting a favorite aunt and uncle at the time . . . Will never forget it, for it changed my life."

"I'd guess it was one of his Social Gospel Trilogy," Arthur broke in.

"Trilogy?" she asked. "There's a trilogy? The one I read was *The Calling of Dan Matthews*, and it really changed my life."

"Oh?" he asked quizzically.

She fumbled a bit for words. "I just don't know how to go on . . . and I don't know yet if . . . if . . . uh . . ."

"If I am a Christian?" he finished for her.

"Yes!"

"Well, I am. Why do you ask?"

"Oh, it's just that *The Calling of Dan Matthews* gave me a new vision of God, of His all-inclusiveness. I'm afraid I had been rather elitist before I read that book."

He laughed, conspiratorially, she thought. "I agree, Miss O'Riley. It hit me that way, too. Only I had read *That Printer of Udels* first—by the way, it anchors the Trilogy—so I was somewhat prepared for his contention that Christ's entire earthly ministry was not about doctrine at all, but about—"

"Service," she broke in softly.

"Yes, service for others," he agreed.

They talked a long time about Wright that day, and after that about other authors of mutual interest. Some they loved in common; others they did their best to convert the other to.

He had always felt he could more than hold his own in any battle of wits, but he discovered that in Jennifer, he had met his match. One day as they sparred back and forth on the historical romances of Rafael Sabatini, they discovered that while each had favorites, both agreed that *Scaramouche*, that great tale of the French Revolution, stood out above all others. He grimaced. *She never misses a trick; not a nuance escapes her!*

During another visit she found a copy of a book she'd searched for for years—Gene Stratton Porter's *The Fire Bird*. She quickly settled into an easy chair in a quiet niche, turned up the lamp, and began leafing through it. She held no illusions about buying it, though. Beautiful and rare, true, but the price was far too high for *her* budget.

Then she heard voices, one of which sounded very familiar. The voices drew nearer, and she pressed her back into the cushion, drawing her legs under her, trying to be as inconspicuous as possible. They sat down in the alcove just before hers, so she couldn't help but overhear.

"I just don't know what I'm going to do, Mr. Bond!" quivered a woman's voice. "I really don't. Lately, I—I—just feel even the good Lord has forsaken me."

"*That*, Mrs. Henry, I can assure you is not true. The Lord *never* forsakes His children," he responded.

"Oh, but Mr. Bond, you just don't *know* or you wouldn't be so sure. My oldest son—you remember Chris? Well, he's on drugs. Worse than that, he's become a pusher." Her voice broke. "And Dana. I—I just found out she's pregnant. I just can't believe it. She grew up so faithful in attending church every week. And the man—the man who, uh—"

"The father of the unborn baby?"

"Yes. He attends our church, too."

"Oh. Are they planning to marry?"

"That's the worst part. He says it's all her fault for not taking precautions. Won't have anything more to do with her. And Dana's near desperate. I'm afraid she'll, she'll—" And again her voice broke.

The other voice broke in, firmly and kindly.

"Mrs. Henry, there is no time to lose. Is Dana home this afternoon?"

When she answered in the affirmative, he led her out and, after explaining to the clerks that an emergency had come up, he and Mrs. Henry hurried through the heavy rain to their cars.

For a long time Jennifer just sat there, thinking. *What kind of bookstore— What kind of man was this?*

She came back within the week and shamelessly stayed within listening range of where he worked. She simply *had* to know for sure who he was. So many times before she'd been disappointed, disillusioned. Why should this one prove to be any different?

She was, by turns, amazed, then moved, by what she overheard. He apparently possessed endless patience for she never heard him lose his temper, no matter what the provocation. Even with bores, who insisted on talking on and on about themselves. She discovered that while most asked book-related questions, a surprisingly large number of people came who felt overwhelmed by life and its problems. In Arthur they found, perhaps not always solutions, but at least a listening, sympathetic ear. In used-book stores, she had discovered, there appears to be an implied assumption: one finds an ear, no matter how stupid, inane, or ridiculous the topic may be. In that respect used-book stores function as courts of last resort, the last chance to be heard before outright despair sets in. But in Arthur's case it went far far beyond mere listening. He genuinely *cared!*

* * *

At last came August, and with it presession.

Vacation was over, for school would begin in a few weeks. She was so busy that it was almost Labor Day before she got back to Pandora's Books. Just as she was leaving he came out of his office and smiled at her. On the confidence of that smile she walked over to him and asked if he could spare a moment.

"Of course!" he replied, and steered her into a quieter room, seating her by an open window. The heat had finally broken, and the cool bay breeze felt like heaven.

After some small talk, she became aware of how strongly this man affected her, this tangible synthesis of strength, wisdom, and kindness. She was more aware of being near him than she had ever been with any other man. Stumbling a bit over her words, she asked him if he ever spoke to students about books, such as in a schoolroom setting.

"Often, Miss O'Riley."

For some unaccountable reason, she blushed. Pandora chose this moment to demand attention and he lifted her up into his arms, where she ecstatically began to purr and knead her claws on his shirt.

"You see, Miss O'Riley," he continued, "since they represent our future, there can be no higher priority than children."

She found herself inviting him to speak to her class, and he gladly accepted.

As she drove home, her Camaro left a trail of greenish-yellow leaves dancing in its wake. She acknowledged that she'd just set forces in motion, forces that might breach almost any wall she'd built up through the years.

Apprehensive she was, a little. But she sang an old love song again and again all the way home, not realizing until her garage door opened on command just what she'd been singing.

* * *

He came with a big box of books and sat down on the floor with the children, holding them enthralled by stories that came from those books and the men and women who illustrated them. And he answered each of the many questions they asked. The ones he couldn't, he promised to answer the day their teacher brought them on a field trip to his wildlife sanctuary/book store, when they could meet Pandora. Jennifer pulled back from her usual focal center to give him the opportunity to be in control. She needn't have bothered: she knew now that when he walked into a room it was as if he was iridescent, for he attracted all eyes as if he shone like the sun. Just as was true (though she didn't know it) of herself.

She watched his every move, listened to his every word, and watched the quicksilver moods as they cavorted on his face and danced in his blue-gray eyes, eyes that held the impishness of the eternal child in them. Like the legendary Pied Piper of Hamlin, the children would have followed him *anywhere*.

And he, though apparently he saw nothing but the children, never missed a nuance of her. The vision she made leaning against the window would hang in the galleries of his mind for all time: a Dante Gabriel Rossetti dream woman. Her long bronze hair, ignited by the late morning sun, her emerald green dress, and her seize-the-day face, added up to far more than mere beauty.

Before he left he let each child choose a favorite book and left the rest for the room library. Then, after reminding them to come see Pandora soon, he was gone, and the halcyon day clouded over. But the sun came back out again when one curious little boy sneaked to the window and caught sight of Mr. Bond getting into his 1957 Thunderbird. His awestruck "Wow!" brought the entire class to the window in seconds, and they all waved. And he, catching the motion at the window, waved back as the coral sand convertible sped out of sight.

But, he hoped, not out of memory. Just to make sure, that afternoon a florist delivered a large autumn floral display, crowned by a couple of book-topped spears. At the very top perched a goldish-brown cat.

That night he called. Did she want to go with him to the Kennedy Center to hear the Vienna Choir Boys? *Was the Pope Catholic?*

Not long after, his second call came, asking her to attend church service with him. After that, the telephone worked both ways. Concerts, galleries and exhibits of the Smithsonian, the opera, rides to the seashore, visits to quaint restaurants in old inns, and hikes along mountain trails—all this brought roses to her cheeks and a glow into her eyes.

After Thanksgiving dinner at her folks, Arthur told her to bundle up for a rather chilly ride. Always, it seemed with him, the car's top stayed firmly down. He reveled in the panoramic view. On and on the Bird sped, and as she nestled down, the excitement brimming over in her eyes and the way her paisley scarf set off her flaming mane of hair made it a struggle to keep his eyes on the road.

The population thinned out as the Bird's deep

throat rumbled into old St. Mary's City. They stopped by the river for a while, ostensibly to watch the geese, but in reality because he felt reflective.

"You know, Jennifer, I think it's time I told you a little more about my failed marriage."

"That's up to you, Arthur."

"How do I start? I had known Marilyn for a number of years; we attended the same parochial high school, same college—even same church. My folks were good friends with her folks—had been for many years. We liked the same things, shared many of the same dreams."

She listened, gazing out at the river.

Arthur laughed a strangely undefinable laugh. "Actually, I don't think I ever proposed—we just drifted into it. All our friends, our families, our folks, took it for granted. So we married. We loved each other. *That*, I'm sure of. It was to be for life, at least it was for *me*." There was a long pause, as he searched for the right words. "We were married about 18 months. Then one never-to-be-forgotten spring morning, after breakfast, she announced that marriage was 'a bore,' 'a drag,' and that she wanted to regain her freedom."

A pause, then in a flat voice, he continued. "So she divorced me and found another—several anothers. That was about 12 years ago, but it seems like yesterday. . . . Oh, I foundered for a time; my self-esteem was at its all-time low." Then he brightened. "But God saw me through. I escaped to the New England coast . . . stayed there a long time, healing. It was there that the epiphany came to me: "Pandora's Books.""

"Oh!" she breathed, half a sigh, half a paean.

"Yes, a dream bookstore, unlike any I had ever seen or heard about. But the Lord showed me that mere business success would not be enough. I must also care for His sheep. *That* would be my ministry. And the frosting on the cake—"

"Was Pandora," Jennifer finished.

"Yes, Pandora," he smiled, started the engine, and they were again out on the highway, heading south.

I'm so glad he told me! she thought, as the Bird gathered speed. *He didn't walk out on her. . . . He had to have been hurt more than I was, yet he didn't let it destroy him. There was closure—a long time ago. . . . There's a clear road ahead! Oh, Lord, thank You!* And her heart began to sing.

She lost all track of time as the Bird raced down the peninsula, leaving waves of gold and crimson leaves in its wake. Suddenly, there was only a narrow gray strip of land ahead, banked by white-capped blue below and white-winged gulls in blue sky above. The car nosed into a parking space at the end of the road. Since it was both cold and blustery, they had it all to themselves.

For a few minutes they just sat there, watching and listening to the gulls. She wondered what he was thinking.

Leaning back, his hands behind his head, he finally broke into her reverie. "You know, Jennifer, this is what I miss most. Solitude. The solitude you can still find out West and up North. So many people live here that, after a while, one gets claustrophobic. At least I do. If anything ever moves me away from this bay it will be that. Well, that and my beloved mountains. I miss them."

Suddenly he shifted in his seat and laughed. "Am I ever the gabby one today! Enough about me. What about *you*? What is *your* story? Hasn't some gallant knight tried to gallop away with you?"

Shyly, she answered, "Y-e-e-s."

"Well, what happened?" he demanded, an impish look in his eyes. "'Fess up; I did my stint, now it's your turn."

So she told him, and took a while doing it. When she finally finished, he sat in silence a while, then smiled. "I'm glad. Someday I may tell you why."

"Someday you may, huh?" she laughed, her eyes narrowing.

"You know, Jennifer, your voice has bells in it. Your laugh, most of all. Even on the phone I hear bells ringing when you speak. You radiate happiness."

She blushed, started to say something, then stopped.

"Go on," he chuckled. "Might as well get it out."

"Oh!" she said, trying to slow her racing heart. "It's just that I've been happy a lot lately and—and"—refusing to meet his eyes—"you're to blame." There. It was out, and her eyes fell, unable to meet his.

Silence thundered in her ears. When at last she looked up, he was looking out to sea, an enigmatic look on his face. His body had tensed, his face was now rigid. She felt utterly humiliated by her admission.

Then he turned, placed his hand on hers butterfly-briefly and said, "Well, it's getting late. What do you say to heading back?"

All the way back she wallowed in misery. *Why did I wreck what had been so perfect? Why change gears when we were just beginning to gain momentum in the lower one?*

Once she caught him eyeing her pensively.

When he walked her to her door, they didn't banter as usual. He didn't ask her for another date, just "Thank you, Jennifer, for a perfect Thanksgiving!" uttered in a flat voice.

That was a long, *long* night for Jennifer. *Stupid me! I've blown it!* she wailed to herself. *I took a wonderful friendship, just beginning to bud, and wrecked it. Might just as well have demanded the full-blown rose! But that's just it: I'm in love with him. Been in love with him for a long time—just refused to admit it.* She sniffed. *He storms me in his quiet, gentle way. I—I've never met anyone before who lights up every room he's in—at least for me. I know it's shameless, but here I am in my 30s, having never known passion (wondering if I even had it in me), and now with this man I yearn for him, long for him,* desire *him with every inch of my body, heart, and soul!*

Her thoughts raced on. *Friendship alone was no longer enough, even if it obviously was for him. My passionate heart cries for far more. I cannot be merely another in a long line of friendships (perhaps even romances) with him. If only I had waited perhaps it would have come. Oh, why, Lord, did I do it! Oh, God, to find my soul's other half after all these long years and then to lose him because of my big big mouth.* And she wept through the endless night.

But when he called, as usual, to ask her to attend church with him, she turned him down in an icy voice, then cut the conversation short by saying, "I'm sorry. Gotta run; I'm late!" Then she *was* miserable, for in reality she had nothing else to do at all and an entire evening to do it in.

* * *

Jennifer loved the Christmas season because it was a time when being a child again became an accepted thing. With what joy she always greeted the wreathes and garlands, the multicolored lights on the neighborhood eaves and trees, the Advent candles, the Christmas trees seen through the windows, the Christmas carols played continuously by radio stations. This year, though, she just wished it would go away. Even in her schoolroom. True, she decorated it in the usual way, drilled the children for the big Christmas program, and helped them make personalized gifts for those dearest to them. But it all seemed hollow, all a sham. She knew it was irrational, but she felt that even God had somehow let her down.

Lord, how could You do this to me? How could You let me make such a fool of myself?

She no longer kidded herself about what Arthur meant to her, or that he could be but a passing fancy that would go away. No, for better or for worse, he'd be a deep-rooted part of her as long as she lived. He did not call again. Several times—no, a hundred times she felt the urge to call him and apologize for her curtness on the phone, but her lacerated pride just would not let her.

Her last papers were corrected and the scores added up. Gifts had been accepted from each of her students and the big program (to which she'd once planned to invite Arthur) went off without a hitch. Yet none of it meant anything to her. Nothing at all.

On that dismal winter evening she simply sat in her not-even-decorated-this-year townhouse, wallowing in misery and self-pity, wishing for him, *yearning* for him, and dreading Christmas week.

Then the phone rang.

She answered it, but no bells rang in her subdued hello. She almost hung up when she heard his voice on the other end, inwardly raging because his voice possessed this power over her, giving her goose bumps. But there was something different in *his* voice, almost a pleading note. He had a big favor to ask of her, he said.

"A favor?" she snapped, and then could have choked her misbehaving self for that snippiness.

Silence swirled around her. Then he continued, more haltingly this time. He had a big favor to ask, yes, but with a qualifier or two thrown in. First of all, he wanted her to share "The Messiah" with him at Washington's National Cathedral. And second, he wanted to show her something that would be of extreme importance to her.

When the silence on the other end of the line continued, he gulped and added, "If you'll accept just this once, I promise not to ever bother you again."

She saw no graceful way out, so she managed an undernourished "Yes."

There. Finished. That would end it. No ellipsis, no dash, no period. *Period, period, period . . . But three periods would be an open-ended ellipsis!* shouted an irrational thought from a far corner of her brain.

Her mind raced, her thoughts milling in chaotic confusion. *I shouldn't have said yes, that I'd go. But I'd hate to miss out on going. . . . I don't think I can handle being close to him again—I'm so sure my face will give me away, if my big mouth doesn't. Yet how can I possibly give up this one last time, the last time we'll ever be together? . . . Oh, it will tear my heart out to be close to him and not be able to touch him! Not to be able— But I don't want him to take anyone else there. Certainly—make that double certainly—*

not that Spanish beauty. What am I going to wear?

The big evening (the *last* evening, she promised herself) finally came. She dressed carefully in her favorite blue gown, a Diane Fries she had purchased from Nordstrom's in a rare fit of recklessness. She'd make it a swan song to remember. Then she put on her heavy black cashmere coat, bought on sale just before I Magnin closed.

The doorbell rang, her pulse quickened. She forced herself to walk very slowly to the door, lest she appear too eager. *Oh, I am despicable!* she chided herself. When she saw him standing there, sapphire stars sparkled in her eyes and crimson color rose in her cheeks, in spite of her well-planned intentions. He was so—so *detestably* dear.

At the curb, its motor purring, was a car she had not seen before. A Mercedes 560, a suspicious shade of emerald green.

"Wouldn't dare park the Bird in D.C." was all he said as he helped her in.

Outside the window, the white of the first snowfall of the year enveloped the world. Christmas CDs played softly through the car's sophisticated sound system, and she relaxed a little, in spite of herself. Neither one said much during the ride to the cathedral.

They had a tough time finding a parking space, but finally joined the well-dressed throng filling the streets. Excitement flooded Jennifer's cheeks, and once or twice she trembled as his hand brushed hers.

All was Christmas inside the world's sixth largest cathedral, and he moved, with her just behind him toward the nave. He took her hand now to keep her close. Eventually they arrived at the spot where he felt the acoustics would be nearly perfect and found a pillar on which to lean, for the seats were all taken.

Then the organ found its voice, shaking the near-century-in-the-making building, and chills went up her spine. Pipe organs had that power over her. She sneaked a sideways glance at him and felt satisfied by the look of awe on his face. The orchestra, the soloists, the choirs . . . She lost all track of time as Handel transported her through the drama of the ages.

Through it all, she remained aware of him, but in a sort of haze. He left once and returned with chairs for both of them. She sank down with a sigh of relief. After a couple hours, unconsciously declaring a temporary truce, she took advantage of his tall frame and leaned her head against him. She felt him tremble when a draft of cold air blew a strand of her flame-colored hair across his face.

Soaring upward, her soul drank deeply of the majesty of the mighty columns and graceful arches that portrayed the architectural yearning for the Eternal. The words and music and organ and choirs and soloists and cathedral set her sensibilities awash in a glorious joy.

During the "Hallelujah Chorus," as she stood at his

side, she again felt him tremble, and peeped sideways to find him wiping away tears. Since she was crying, too, she felt a renewed sense of kinship with him. The crowd was unbelievably quiet as they found their way out, almost as if words seemed far too fragile to accommodate such divine freight.

On the slippery road again, neither spoke, and the sound system remained silent, as if anything else right now would be anticlimactic. For this she inwardly thanked him, for his sensitivity and empathy, for not shattering the mood. So surreal was it all that she didn't even notice they had passed her exit until the Mercedes veered off Highway 50 onto Riva Road.

To her raised eyebrows, he merely smiled and said,. "Remember, there's more to this promised evening."

The traffic thinned south of Annapolis, and the flocked evergreens flashed by. Slowly, haltingly, he began to speak. "Undoubtedly, you—you, uh, wondered about my strange response to your—to what you said about yourself the last time we were together."

She stiffened. *How dare he bring up that utterly humiliating afternoon, when he rejected my stupid disclosure of my inner feelings.*

But he plowed on, not looking at her. "You see, Jen"—he'd never called her by her family pet name before—"I was so wounded, so scarred, by the rejection I told you about that I determined that never again . . ." He struggled for control, then continued. "Never again would I let a woman get that close to me."

He paused, and she hardly dared breathe.

"But it's been hard, Jen, because I'm still young—and lonely. It's been very hard."

"The beautiful black-haired girl who works for you?" She couldn't help herself.

He almost hit a tree, but when he turned toward her his face had relaxed just a little. "How did you know?"

"I have eyes. Any woman could have told you."

There was a long silence as he searched for the right words. Finally, as if he had given up searching for any better ones, he returned to the refrain again. "It's been hard." But he did not tell her that it was the Spanish beauty's lack of tenderness, her repulsing of the little crying boy, that had turned the tide of his life. Neither did he tell her about the effect *she* had made on him that same day: a Raphael madonna, tenderly holding a child.

After a time, he continued. "You see, Jen, I could not take such rejection twice in one lifetime. I'm afraid it would, well, destroy me!" He paused again. "Marriage for me is for life, even if our society seems to disagree with me." His words seemed sadly bitter to the wondering woman at his side. "And marriage without God to cement it is dead-end. I don't see how any marriage can last a lifetime without a higher power to anchor in. All around me I see marriage after marriage, live-in relationships galore, collapse, so few making it through. I have been afraid. I'm not ashamed to admit it, Jen. I've been terribly afraid to even consider marriage again."

She remained silent. Numb.

"As for children and what divorce or separation does to them . . . There are simply no words in the dictionary terrible enough to fully describe the damage to them, to their feelings of self-worth. I see it every day. And I don't yet know what to do, what to say, to their anguish—anguish so intense it's long since wrung out all the tears they can cry."

And she, remembering those lonely, deeply-scarred, wounded ones in her classes could only nod her head.

"And then *you* came," he said. "You scared me."

He caught her whispered *"Scared?"*

"Yes, scared. Because you were, well, what I never had, yet had always wanted. In a way, too good to be true. Jen, I never expected to find such a woman as you. So when you told me last Thanksgiving that I— that I made you happy, like an absolute fool, I panicked! I had blocked such a future out of the realm of the possible for so many years that when it came, I just, just didn't know how—"

Suddenly he slowed and turned down a familiar road, now a fairyland in the snow. Her heart began to thud so loudly she felt certain he must surely hear it. Then he turned down another road and made a long, wide turn. There, directly ahead in a blaze of holiday lights, stood Pandora's Books.

Her hands flew to her face in breathless surprise. She didn't see his relieved smile.

Inside, festive music played in every room, only all the same track this time. Christmas decorations were everywhere, lights and trees of various sizes.

"I've always loved Christmas. Guess I never grew up," he said simply.

She reached for his hand. He showed her each room, and her delighted response and the restored bells in her voice were all he could have hoped for. Finally, they came back to the office area, and he stepped briefly behind the counter, where he must have flipped a

switch, for suddenly silence shattered the mood, and she was alone with him in the big building.

He walked back to her and she raised her emerald eyes to his, seeking something that had not been there before. Then she heard music again and stood very still. *"Étude in E,"* she whispered.

"Yes."

"Why, Arthur? I don't understand what you're trying to—"

Softly placing his finger on her lips he whispered, "Listen!"

She listened. And, as she knew it would (it always had), it melted her. And, as she knew she would (she always had), she cried. Sudden fire blazed through her tears, and she accused, "How could you! You *know* how that affects me. I saw you watching me that day."

Know? Yes, he knew. *It's all come down to this question, this moment,* he thought. *I hurt her terribly by my inexcusable fear of commitment, and now I must answer. And this is no time for half-hearted measures. But words are such inadequate things! How can I make* her *know?*

Gathering her in his arms, he answered softly, "I just *had* to, dear . . . dearest."

Her wounded pride struggled to assert itself. *How dare he assume I'd forgive him this easily for the hell he put me through? How* dare *he?*

In the end, her pride lost. Gentle he remained, but as immovable as Gibraltar. The *Étude* was on his side, too. It was two against one. She felt her resistance ebbing. Then she made the mistake of trying to read the expression on his face, not easy, considering the dim lighting in the room. But what she saw there closed forever all avenues of escape: Love undiluted, unqualified, undistilled, unreserved, undivided. His heart was empty of all else but *her*.

All the lights of the world came on in her eyes, and her arms stole up and closed behind his neck. All shackles of fear and regret fell clanging to the floor. He started to tell her how much he loved her, but she, cutting his words off with her lips, showed him a better way. A far better way.

Some time later, he sensed a familiar presence at his ankles. Looking down, but not releasing her from the prison of his arms by so much as one link, he smiled. "Sorry, Pandora, you jealous ol' thing. From now on you're just gonna have to *share!*"

* * *

Afterword: I think I've been preparing to write this story all my life. Each of the thousands of used-book stores I've known (many that I've loved) represent the gestation period. Part of the mix is the Haunted Bookstore in Annapolis, Maryland, where Mike, the big tabby cat, undisputedly ruled its premises. Occasionally, he could even be found sleeping in the display window. Sadly, Mike and that wonderful bookstore no longer grace Maryland's capital city, owing to the escalating of the rent. And there is some of Christopher Morley's wonderful book, The Haunted Bookshop, stirred in, as well. Actually, the story represents a synthesis of my own dream bookstore, had I the money and time to make it happen.

Étude in E is considered by many to be the most beautiful étude ever composed. Chopin dedicated it to his dear friend, Franz Liszt, and it remained Chopin's personal favorite of all his own études. Norman Luboff recorded it in perhaps as romantic a recording as has ever been made, in his Reverie album.

And the deeply wounded Jennifer and Arthur. Each of us knows them personally, for they represent a far too large part of our love-'em-and-leave-'em-and-never-count-the-cost society.

As for Pandora, in real life she is Pandora, the pampered Himalayan who has ruled our book-laden house for nearly 10 years now. Life without that furry presence, that constant companion, that flopper-against-me every time I sit or lie down or try to write something worth reading, is too unthinkable to even consider. But always, in this story, she will live on.